THE SHADY SIDE

SHORTCUT TO UNEASY STREET

The Uneasy Series
Volume II

THE SHADY SIDE

SHORTCUT TO UNEASY STREET

Second Edition

SHANNON RAE NOBLE

Text Copyright © 2018 Shannon Rae Noble

Volume II of The Uneasy Series
The Shady Side:
Shortcut to Uneasy Street

First Edition Printing 2018
Second Edition Printing September, 2024

All rights reserved. No part of this publication may be reproduced, distributed, or transmitted in any form or by any means, including photocopying, recording, or other electronic or mechanical methods, without the prior written permission of the publisher, except in the case of brief quotations embodied in critical reviews and certain other noncommercial uses permitted by copyright law.

This book is a work of fiction. Names, characters, places, and incidents either are products of the author's imagination or are used fictitiously. Any resemblance to actual persons, living or dead, events, or locales is entirely coincidental. Some of these stories have been previously published online.

Cover art by Taylor Alyson Butchko
@tayloralysonart

Published by:

Crow 99 Books
PO Box 295
Port Crane, NY 13833

info@crow99books.com

ISBN: 978-1-7321793-6-3

For Matthew and Stephanie.

TABLE OF CONTENTS

Shady Lane	1
Lacey Skipped Home	20
Helena	30
Defensive Driving	40
A Brand-New Girl	82
Wrath	103

SHADY LANE

Tony toweled off quickly and pulled on a clean pair of shorts and a T-shirt. He brushed his teeth, tugged a comb through his short black hair, and stuffed his last-minute hygiene essentials into his duffle bag. He only had thirty minutes to get to the bus station, and he was hoofing it. He grabbed the duffle and slung it onto his shoulder.

He felt his pocket for his wallet, opened it to make sure he still had cash for his bus ticket. He checked for his lucky lighter, the Zippo that Dario had given him.

He picked his way over crushed beer cans and empty pizza boxes, not bothering to be quiet. His roommates were passed out cold, anyway.

The stifling heat of the summer morning struck Tony full in the face as he let the screen door slam behind him. By the time he'd walked two blocks, his shirt was clinging to his back and drops of sweat trickled down his legs.

Tony's empty stomach began to roll and he nearly retched when the stink of exhaust rose from the street, combining with the intense heat and surrounding him like a dirty wall.

Should have taken a cab, he thought.

He wished he were already home.

He hitched the duffle bag higher on his shoulder. Arriving at the Main Street intersection, he decided he could still make the bus on time if he stopped into The Corner Café to grab a couple of donuts and some extra snacks. The food should be just enough to get him through the four-hour bus ride.

He emerged a few moments later with a half-dozen donuts, a bag of chips, several smoked beef jerky sticks, two sandwiches – ham and Swiss - and a couple of bottles of water.

He bit greedily into one of the donuts, its fresh sponginess melting in his mouth, and chased it with some of the water. The initial bite stopped his turning stomach with the promise of more sustenance. Unzipping his duffle, he stuffed in the paper bag with his sandwiches and other snacks and slung it back over his shoulder.

He checked the time on his cell phone. Crap! He had to get moving or he'd miss the bus.

He picked up the pace to make up the few minutes he had lost, finishing off the donut as he went.

The soles of his sneakers hit the cement sidewalk as he turned the corner onto Shady Lane, his arms pumping back and forth. He ignored the passing scenery to his left and right, focusing on the far end of Shady Lane, kitty-corner from where the bus station was located. As he hurried along, he replayed the telephone conversation he'd had with his mother that morning.

He'd awakened to his Lamb of God ringtone blasting from his cell phone at 5:04 a.m.

"Hi Momma, what's up? Is everything okay?"

"Antonio!" Olivia Coronado's voice sounded distressed, like she had been crying.

THE SHADY SIDE

Tony sat up in bed. "Momma? What is it? What's wrong?"

He heard her inhale deeply. "Your father and brother were in a car accident when they were coming home from work this morning. I'm calling from the hospital."

"Are they okay?"

"Your father is stable. His face is bruised up and very swollen. He has three broken ribs and his left knee is shattered. He is sleeping now."

"What about Dario?"

A pause, then a sob from the other end of the line. "Your brother is in critical condition. He's lost a lot of blood. The doctors aren't sure that he will make it. We're waiting." Her voice clogged. She cleared her throat. "Can you come?"

"I'm on the next bus out, Momma."

"What about school?"

"Doesn't matter. I'm done, took my finals yesterday. Wouldn't matter anyway, I would still come."

Tony didn't have much use for his old man. He had been a heavy-fisted drunk when Tony was growing up; that is, when he'd been around.

But he needed to get home to his big brother.

Dario had lived a fast life. He'd been in and out of jail since he was old enough to be incarcerated, and had done the dance with alcohol and drugs. At twenty-five, he had nearly died from a heroin overdose. Dario had been lucky, though, and he had survived long enough to take hold of his tattered life and try to repair it – and himself.

Despite Dario's personal issues, he had always taken care of Tony. When their old man pulled the belt off, ready to go at Tony, Dario shielded his little brother and took it for him. When Tony was bullied at school, Dario knocked the shit out of Tony's tormentors, who quickly learned to leave Tony alone.

When the old man disappeared for days at a time and their mom was gone at work or laid up in bed with depression and migraines, Dario played mom *and* dad, making sure that Tony was fed, clean, and that he went to school and did his homework.

Sitting on the front stoop one autumn day, passing time with Dario, the boom box blaring, watching traffic go by, Tony had said, "Dario, how come you do so much stuff for me? How come you don't pick on me like the other guys pick on their little brothers?"

Dario had contemplated him with a serious expression in his liquid dark brown eyes. The jagged white scar under his left eye that their father had given him one evening with a beer bottle glared out. His thick black hair, pulled into a sleek ponytail, gleamed in the bright afternoon sunlight.

He took a drag off the non-filtered Lucky Strike he was smoking, tapped the ash, and stared across the street at the bags of trash piled up on the porch of the Bransons' house, which looked like it was about to cave in behind its chain-link fence. Flies buzzed around the pile of trash bags. A mangy dog rooted among them, looking for food.

"Who else is gonna take care of you?" he said. "Mom and Dad don't do shit. They never took care of me, they don't take care of you. Around here, the parents don't care, they live in their own little worlds. Drunk dads, moms on oxy, sleepin' life away 'cause their life is shit. Everybody's on some kind of drug. You name it, there it is. Families are supposed to look out for one another, but in this neighborhood, it's everyone for himself. They give up."

He took a last drag from his cigarette and flicked the butt into the gutter. He looked at Tony again. "You know those TV shows? The dramas and sitcoms, with all the brothers and sisters, mom and dad and the housekeeper? The families, they all stick together. They talk shit out.

That happens some places. It's real, but not here. Shit can grow flowers, though. Just because we're born here, we don't need to stay. There's a better life for you. Don't want to be like all these other assholes, livin' and dyin' in the trash heap. I don't want to push you down. I want to push you out of here."

He turned his lighter over and over with his fingers. It was a stainless steel Zippo with a Celtic cross etched into both sides. The cross had once been painted black, but the paint had chipped and worn away. The lighter was scratched and dented from years of use and abuse. He suddenly held it out to Tony.

"Here. That was my last cigarette. I quit. I'm done with everything. Take my lucky lighter, and don't say I never gave you nothin'. I been a shitty role model. I don't want to be like the old man."

"But I don't smoke."

"You can use a lighter for stuff besides smokin'. You never know when you might need a good flame to light somethin' up." He reached out and smacked Tony on the back of his head, hard enough to sting.

"Ow! What you do that for?"

"Don't tell nobody what I just said. You'll wreck my rep. Mouth shut, right?"

* * *

Still walking briskly, Tony uncapped his water bottle and took a few large gulps. As he twisted the cap back on, he nearly fell when he tripped over something that made dry clicking sounds.

He looked down. At his feet lay a small pile of what looked like little white knobby, polished tree branches mixed with bits of red cotton fluff. He squatted to see better. A chill slid down his spine when he realized he was looking at a tiny rib cage and the skull of a small animal, surrounded by the rest of its skeleton. The red cotton fluff was bloody fur. The remains looked like those of a cat.

Tony straightened up and looked around, viewing Shady Lane with sudden clarity.

The neighborhood, with its green, well-manicured lawns, various garden décor and porch flowers in red, pink, blue, and white, was quiet. A slight breeze rustled the foliage of the trees that lined the sidewalks on either side of the street. There was an occasional vehicle parked here and there beside the curb, but no moving traffic – cars, bicyclists, or pedestrians, other than Tony, himself.

He stepped over the small pile of bones and moved forward, more slowly this time. He tried to convince himself that there was nothing creepy going on.

Maybe Shady Lane is just quiet this morning. People are slow getting up and around. Maybe that dead animal is just a cat that was mauled by a dog, he thought.

Tony's thoughts trailed off and he stopped again when he saw the grisly scene that lay before him.

To his left, a teal colored Subaru Forester sat in the driveway of a large white house. Beside the vehicle, a bright green garden hose lay on the asphalt, water running steadily from the nozzle. The thick hose snaked up to the finger bones of the hand that still gripped the trigger handle. The hand was attached to the arm bone that protruded from the tattered sleeve of a dark blue T-shirt. Tony could see rib bones peeking through the torn fabric, across which a dark stain had spread. A human skull lolled on the asphalt above the collar of the shirt. Tufts of short brownish hair stuck to whatever pieces of scalp remained. The leg bones were intact, sticking out of a bloody, shredded pair of khaki shorts. The flip-flops the man had been wearing lay, carelessly discarded, a few feet away.

A faint *ding ding ding* noise caught Tony's attention. He looked across the street and saw an older red Ford

THE SHADY SIDE

Tempo parked at the curb. Its driver side door was open, and a skeleton wearing a bloody blue and white print sundress knelt on its knobby skeleton knees, its upper half resting on the driver side seat. He guessed that the "ding" noise was the car's "door open" reminder.

He looked past the Tempo to the house beyond it. The contents of two paper grocery bags had spilled across the house's front porch and down the steps. Shiny red bones adorned with scraps of muscle and flesh lay among scattered cans of tomato sauce and vegetables, boxes of macaroni elbows and Raisin Bran, a six-pack of Pepsi, a loaf of bread, and various other food items.

Up ahead, on his side of the street, lay the four-legged remains of a dog. Tony knew it was a dog because a collar still encircled its neck, clipped to a leash held by the small human companion that lay crumpled on the sidewalk beside its pet.

Everywhere he looked, Tony saw carnage: a human or an animal, the meat picked from the bones, which reflected, red and glossy with smeared blood, against the early June sunshine.

Icy fingers of fear radiated from the pit of Tony's stomach and spread upward through his chest. He could hear the blood pulsing through his ears to the rhythmic percussion of his heart. For a split second, he felt like he had passed through the walls of his body, and in a dreamlike state, was looking down upon himself, standing on the sidewalk.

Then he fell back into himself and knew only one thing: he had to get off Shady Lane. He needed to get to the bus station. Screw this street, screw the dead bodies. He didn't want to find out what had happened to all of these people, to the animals. He sure didn't want to stick around long enough to become a casualty, himself.

The bus station is right there, he thought. *Two blocks up.*

He quietly pulled his phone from his pocket; the tiny digital numbers in the corner read 8:37 am. Time to go. Time to go *now*.

When a rustling sound came from a hedge across the street, he paused in the middle of his next step, one foot suspended in the air. He jumped and his heart skipped a panicked beat when something orange burst from the evergreen bushes and streaked toward him.

He laughed weakly when he saw that the creature was a cat. An orange cat with a white stomach and white fur on each paw, like socks. It reached the nearest tree and clawed its way up the trunk, where it disappeared into the ripe green foliage.

Stupid cat.

The cat had come and gone so quickly that the silence that ensued in the animal's wake left Tony questioning whether he had even seen the feline, at all.

The hedge across the street rustled again. Tony stared at the bushes. He swore he could hear a faint buzzing noise coming from that direction. He strained his ears. *Bees?*

No.

He watched, mesmerized, as a stream of tiny creatures poured from the bushes, following the route the cat had just taken. He blinked, wondering if his eyes were playing tricks on him.

At first glance, they looked like naked six-inch tall human beings. Closer inspection revealed a lack of toes on the feet; or else the feet were just so small Tony couldn't see the toes. Their little legs looked as though they were backward-jointed at the knee. The creatures' tiny hands seemed to end in three curved talons; kind of like sloth claws.

As they neared, Tony could see more details of their miniscule faces. Their eyes were narrow and black, slanting in at nearly vertical angles from their nostrils, which were also positioned vertically in the centers of their faces. There was no "nose" in the human sense; just the nostrils. Their faces lacked eyebrows. From their round, snarling mouths protruded long, needle-like teeth.

They came fast, streaming past Tony, up the tree trunk and among the branches where the cat had disappeared.

He heard a hiss and then warning moan of the angry feline, which quickly rose and split the air in an unearthly scream of pain that cut off abruptly. Clumps of blood-stained orange and white fur floated down from the tree's thick foliage.

Tony stood for a moment, paralyzed with shock, fear, and disbelief. He began to back away. He only managed two steps before the creatures started to drop from the tree and swarm after him.

Several of them jumped on his bare legs, anchoring their sharp claws into his flesh, climbing his legs. He screamed, feeling the talons and needle-like teeth sinking deep into the muscles of his calves and thighs. He slapped at them, and, looking up, he saw more of them coming in what seemed like an endless wave.

He realized he couldn't just stand there and let them chew him up right where he stood, like they had chewed up and spit out the residents of Shady Lane.

He swung his tightly-packed duffle bag back and forth in front of him, sending bunches of the creatures flying in large *poofs* of bloody chunks and tissue spray.

He turned and ran back to the driveway where the Forester was parked, dislodging a few of the little monsters. He bent down, yanked the green hose handle from the dead man's fingers, hoisted his duffle behind his right shoulder, and squeezed the trigger.

He aimed first at the creatures that still clung to his legs, tearing at his skin and muscle with their teeth. They emitted squeals and shrieks as the force of the water blew them apart. Their bodies slid down Tony's legs in slimy pieces.

"*Aaaahhhhhh!*" The involuntary war cry started in his belly and escaped from his mouth. His terror, transformed now to anger, fueled him. Adrenaline pumped through his body as he swept the hose spray back and forth before him into the swarm of creatures. Some of them flattened into the asphalt in small chunky red puddles. The bright sunlight beamed into the water spray, creating a rainbow, beyond which the spray turned red and pink as he blew more creatures backward and to each side, killing and crippling them.

But they kept coming.

Tony looked behind him and saw the open garage door. He backed up, sweeping the spray to and fro in front of him until he was in the garage. He dropped the hose, reached up, and yanked the garage door down. A few of the creatures got caught beneath the edge of the door and were crushed or cut in half. Some of them made it into the cool, dim space with Tony.

"*No fucking way!*" Tony threw down his duffle and ripped away a couple more of the creatures that had climbed up beneath his shorts. He threw them down and went after the others that had slipped into the garage with him. He stomped blindly, feeling the small, soft bodies give beneath the soles of his sneakers. He heard little crunching noises as their tiny bones broke.

"Take *that!* And *that!*" he screamed. "Does that taste good, *now*? I'm not your fucking lunch!"

After a couple of minutes, Tony realized that he was just stomping around in a puddle of sludge and tiny bones. A gamey, musky smell, mingled with the coppery scent of blood, rose into the air around him.

He stopped, panting. Sweat rolled down his forehead, into his eyes. He could feel it trickling down his back.

THE SHADY SIDE

"*Shit!*" He limped away from the crushed and broken pile of creatures to a clean spot on the garage floor, taking his duffle with him.

He tipped his head back and took a few deep breaths. Then his body started to tremble with shock. He sank to the cool cement floor and tears came, unbidden. He did not want them, but he couldn't stop them. Alone in a stranger's dim garage, Tony sobbed.

"You *fucks*. You little *fucks*!" He rocked back and forth. Those little monsters had cost him his ride to see his brother. Who even knew if Dario was still alive, right now?

His eyes slowly adjusted to the dimness. He used the hem of his T-shirt to wipe his face, hands, and eyes. "*Fuck it.*" He blew his nose on it, too.

Dario would have a shit fit if he saw that. So would Momma.

The thought brought Tony back to the moment, and he cleared this throat. *Get your shit together, wuss. Figure out what you're gonna do.*

He limped over to a series of small square patches of light on the cement floor that beamed through the garage door windows. He examined his wounds.

Tiny rivers of blood ran down his legs from beneath his shredded blood and water-soaked cargo shorts. Small flaps of skin hung from his legs in a dozen places. One flap of skin that had been partially torn from the calf of his right leg was larger and more worrisome. It was almost two inches long.

He couldn't differentiate the many pain sites from one another; the entire surface of each of his legs felt like one huge throbbing, stinging mess.

Tony could hear the sharp nails of the little monsters scratching at the garage door. He grabbed his duffle and slung it over his shoulder. He limped to the door that joined the garage to the house. Conscious of the frustrated, high-pitched, buzzing cacophony of the tiny creatures' voices outside, he tried the knob. It turned, and Tony cautiously pushed the door. Silent on its well-oiled hinges, it swung open easily. He stepped into a shiny white kitchen. He pulled the door closed firmly behind him and turned the lock.

A light breeze moved the sheer, buttercup-yellow curtains at the open windows above the sink. He limped to the sink and leaned against it for a moment, closing his eyes. He could almost smell the sunlight that shone in through the window. He reached up, pulled the window closed, and latched it. He stood for a few seconds longer, listening for the little monsters. Beyond the hum of the refrigerator, he could hear them, but faintly. He noticed a small flat-screen television set mounted on the kitchen wall.

He considered calling out to see whether there were any living inhabitants inside the house, but he decided against it. He didn't want to announce his whereabouts to the mini-monsters.

If anyone is alive in here, I guess I'll find out soon enough.

With each painful step, he sucked his breath in between clenched teeth. He left a bright red trail of blood across the immaculate white tile floor as he limped out of the kitchen and through a hallway in search of a bathroom where he could clean up. He wanted to at least rinse his wounds or, better yet, find some kind of antiseptic. Who knew what kind of diseases those mini-monsters carried?

Tony secured the front door. He checked each room along the way, ensuring that all of the windows were closed and locked.

The third and last door on the left proved to be a bathroom, decorated with a blue color scheme. Blue-painted walls. Blue bath rug, toilet seat cover. Blue patterned shower curtain with matching toothbrush holder, cup, and trash can.

He rifled through the cupboards and found a first aid kit.

Dispensing with all decorum, Tony stripped off his shorts and boxers and ran warm water into the bathtub. Using some Axe body wash he found in the tub and wincing at the re-awakened stinging, he washed his wounds well. He carefully patted his skin dry with a blue towel he pulled from the towel bar.

There was no antibiotic ointment or antiseptic in the first aid kit, but he found a roll of gauze. Tony quietly lowered the toilet seat lid and sat upon the blue plush cover. He tended to the big wound on his calf, holding the dangling flap of skin in place as he wrapped it snugly. He donned a fresh pair of shorts and a clean t-shirt he pulled from his duffle.

He contemplated the thickly carpeted staircase, trying to decide if it was worth it to search upstairs for survivors. He wondered if there might be any mini-monsters hanging around on the second floor.

If there are any mini-monsters inside the house, I would already have met them, he thought. *Won't hurt just to check. Maybe I'll find something that will help me get out of here.*

Because he still needed to get home.

Leaving his bag at the bottom of the staircase, he started climbing the steps, his wounded legs protesting stiffly.

At first, Tony's sneakered feet were silent in the thickly piled carpet. But then the wooden floor creaked loudly beneath the plush covering. The sound was like a gunshot in a library.

Tony stopped and listened. He didn't hear the swarm coming.

Yet.

Stepping gingerly, he ascended one more riser. He discovered that the outside edge of each step was less creaky than the middle, so he began picking his way up the right edge of the stairs.

He thought about calling the police, but discarded the idea. Any kind of vehicle stopping on Shady Lane today would just attract the mini-monsters, who would make short work of a cop or two. If Tony called 911, everyone would show up – fire trucks, paramedics, cops. The bloodthirsty creatures would swarm and overwhelm the first responders.

And if he tried to call 911, what kind of reception would his story be met with, in the first place? Miniature humanoid monsters ate an entire street's worth of residents?

They would think he was either pranking them or high on an acid trip.

What about an exterminator? Animal Control?

There's an idea. But Tony knew these creatures weren't your garden variety wild animal, and imagined that if he tried to explain what they were, he would receive the same response as he would if he called 911. He could lie and say they were rats; but then the individuals arriving upon the scene wouldn't be adequately prepared to deal with the bloodthirsty horde of mini-monsters.

He knew he would have to call for help, but he couldn't, yet. He would just be endangering more people. He had to think of a way out of this house and off of Shady Lane on his own.

The upstairs rooms were empty of humans, dead or alive. As he moved from window to window, making sure each was secured, Tony peered out, trying to pinpoint where the creatures were.

From one of the front bedroom windows, he saw the gaggle of mini-monsters gathered in a group on the front

THE SHADY SIDE

lawn. He could just barely hear their buzzing voices. He watched as they engaged in what looked like an animated conversation. A couple of them gesticulated with their tiny arms. After a couple of minutes, the horde split into three smaller groups, two of which disappeared around opposite sides of the house. The remaining group spread out along the front of the house, but they moved in so close to the exterior walls that Tony lost sight of them. If he opened the window and poked his head out to see what they were doing, he might attract their attention.

No doubt they were seeking a means of entry. He decided to leave it for now. Let them look. He had to devise a plan of escape.

He sat on the bed and pulled out his cell phone. He woke it up and silenced the ringer. He sure didn't need *that* going off. He checked the time; it was nearly 9:05. He'd missed the bus by fifteen minutes. He groaned. *"Fuuuck."*

What would Dario do? Tony pocketed his phone and pulled out the Zippo his brother had given him. Dario's voice repeated in Tony's memory: *"You can use a lighter for stuff besides smokin'. You never know when you might need a good flame to light somethin' up."* The memory made Tony smile. It also set off a chain reaction of thoughts that, like dominoes, clicked as they fell into line. *Bonfires. Big bonfires. Fires. Explosions.*

Hmmm.

A persistent scratching noise gradually broke through his reverie. He looked toward the sound. It came from a heat vent in the corner of the room.

More scratching, scrabbling noises coming from overhead. The sound grew in volume and intensity.

Shit! They got into the vents – and the attic!

Resting time was over.

He needed to be swift and silent. Not sure how well he would manage either, Tony moved.

He found he was able to move quickly, albeit stiffly, despite his injuries. The four years of physical training as he had worked toward his major in athletics had strengthened his muscles; and even though a few of his wounds were nasty, the creatures' teeth and claws had failed to penetrate very deeply into them.

He followed the hallway wall toward the stairs. He propped himself with the railing as he descended, stepping carefully on the outer edge of each carpeted riser. At the bottom, he stopped to listen.

The scratching noises had all but receded, but he didn't trust the silence. He knew that the horde would swarm downstairs in just a few short seconds.

He picked up his bag where he had left it at the base of the stairs, slung it over his shoulder, and entered the kitchen. He lifted the lid off the gas stove and blew out the pilot light for each burner. He located and extinguished the oven pilot light, as well. He then opened up all the gas controls to the oven and the burners.

He thought he'd seen a red plastic can of gasoline in the garage. He stealthily exited the kitchen into the garage, crossing his fingers, hoping that there was still gasoline in the can.

Dust-mote laden shafts of light beamed through the garage door windows onto the concrete floor. The bright sunbeams made the outlying dimness that much darker, leaving the corners in deep shadow.

Tony found the gas can. He hefted it, shook it, and heard the satisfying echo of liquid sloshing against the plastic interior.

He limped back into the kitchen. He dumped some of the gasoline into the oven and quietly shut the oven door. He splashed some of it onto the kitchen floor and left a trail of it out the kitchen door to the garage.

Entering the kitchen one last time, he quickly opened cabinet doors, his eyes scanning past plates and cups, canned and dry goods. *There!* He grabbed a square plastic food storage container and lid. He unzipped his bag just enough to fit them through the opening and stuffed them both inside.

With another brief search, he located the remote control to the flat-screen television. Standing in the doorway to the garage, he clicked the power button on the remote. He turned up the volume and left the remote on the kitchen table. He turned the lock and closed the kitchen door silently behind him.

He grabbed the gasoline can and continued to lay his trail into the garage and across the cement floor. Rather than make a lot of noise by raising the large overhead door, Tony slipped through the access door that opened onto the front walk, after making sure that none of the mini-monsters were outside this part of the house.

He used all the gasoline in the can, splashing it down the front walk, avoiding the water-soaked driveway. When it was empty, Tony set the can down on the front lawn.

He could hear a faint buzzing noise coming from the direction of the living room. Through the sheer white curtains hung at the downstairs windows, he could see the edge of the stair rail where it rose to the second floor, and the dark shadow of a river of mini-monsters racing and tumbling down the stairs. He could also see the glow of the flat-screen television through the buttercup-yellow curtains that covered the kitchen windows.

Time was running out.

He dropped his duffle on the front walk and quickly removed the plastic food storage container. He ran to the scene of carnage in the driveway where he had fended off many of the mini-monsters. He found two or three of the tiny creatures that were still mostly intact, and used the container lid to gingerly lift the bodies up and flip them into the container. He sealed the container and pulled his cell phone from his pocket. He snapped several pictures of the dead creatures in the driveway and took a few more of the human and animal skeletons that littered the street. With what he was about to do, he would need some kind of evidence to back up his story.

If he was asked.

Gagging and looking away, Tony squatted beside the skeleton that lay in the driveway. He dug into its shorts pocket and found a set of keys.

He ran back to his bag and quickly stowed the plastic container. He could hear the horde; the noise was louder. He was sure that the majority of the creatures were now in the kitchen.

He flipped open the lid on the Zippo and drew his thumb across the wheel. The lighter threw a spark, but didn't ignite. He tried again, then again; the smell of butane mingled with the gasoline fumes that surrounded him.

The flame would not take.

Prickles of sweat broke out on Tony's skin. He pushed down the seeds of fear and disappointment. He smacked the lighter against his thigh.

"*Ah!*" he cried. He had forgotten about the many fresh wounds on his legs.

Hundreds of tiny heads inside the house turned in Tony's direction.

He blinked away the sudden tears of pain that blurred his eyes.

He tried his thumb against the lighter's wheel one more time.

The flame ignited.

Tony dropped the flaming lighter into the stream of gasoline he had dumped. He turned and limped as fast as he could toward the Subaru Forester parked in the driveway as the flame followed the stream beneath the access door, inside the garage, and into the kitchen.

Tony tossed his bag into the Forester's passenger seat and slid in behind the steering wheel, slamming the door behind him.

Warumph! The oven ignited and exploded in the kitchen.

Tony found the key, started the vehicle, and slammed it into reverse. Tires screeching, he backed out of the driveway and drove away.

He considered driving the Forester all the way home, but thought better of it. He had just blown up a house on Shady Lane. It might not be a good idea to steal a vehicle, as well. A quick ride to the bus station would suffice.

The two-block drive took less than sixty seconds.

He hadn't spilled any gasoline on himself, but he used the bus terminal restroom to wash up, as he still had bits of blood and gore on his shirt, arms, face, and in his hair.

Just before he climbed aboard the 9:20 bus and safely seated himself, he called 911 to report the loud explosion on Shady Lane.

LACEY SKIPPED HOME

Lacey Lancaster slipped between the padlocked gates of the chain-link fence that bordered the parking lot of the Bric-A-Brac building. Cutting across the sizeable square of pavement with its faded white-painted lines that once denoted parking spaces, she gazed up at the abandoned brick building. It sat, a hulking monolith, its broken windows seeming to stare back at her, pleading for her to stay a while and keep it company. Lacey thought that a building with a name so happy shouldn't look so sad. It exuded an air of loneliness so palpable that by the time she climbed through the hole in the chain-link fence on the far side of the parking lot, she felt very melancholy, indeed.

It was a shortcut she used every day on her way to and from school in the mornings and afternoons. She also used the shortcut to go to her friend Holly's after school and on weekends.

Lacey was on her way home from Holly's house now, and she was stomping mad at her friend. She made angry eyebrows and her little face twisted up like she had just

THE SHADY SIDE

tasted a lemon as she muttered to herself in a snotty mimic of her friend's voice. "It's *my* house, so we have to play what *I* want to play. It's *my* game, so we have to play the way *I* want. They're *my* dolls, so I get to pick which one I get to play with, and *you* get to play with whatever's left over. Ugh! Holly is *so* bossy! *And* unfair," she added. In fact, Holly wasn't much of a friend. Everything always had to be *her* way. "Next time we're gonna play *my* way, or I won't be her friend anymore!"

A lone stray kitten ran from one of the outer entrance doorways of the building. It trotted up to Lacey and meowed plaintively. Lacey forgot her anger. Her expression softened as she squatted to pet the kitten's fluffy, dove-gray fur. "Aw, hi! Where do you live? Do you have a house?" The kitten rubbed its tiny face against her ankles. Its whiskers tickled her skin. "I wish I could take you home, but my mom and dad won't let me have a kitty. Not until I get older. Oohh, you're so soft!"

After petting the kitten quietly for a moment, Lacey said, "I wish I had some food to give you. I'm sorry though, I have to go home." The sun was sinking in the sky and shadows were growing long. "I have to be home by dinner time or I'll get in trouble. Hey, I'll find some food and if you're here tomorrow, I'll give it to you!"

She stood and began skipping across the parking lot. Home was only four blocks away, but she knew she had to hustle.

The kitten ran ahead of her as though it knew where she was going and intended to beat her there. It stopped to lick itself, fell behind, then ran ahead again for several feet. It disappeared into a shadow that stretched across the pavement at the far end of the parking lot.

Lacey skipped forward, expecting to see the kitten emerge from the opposite side of the dark space into the late afternoon sunshine; but the kitten failed to reappear.

Lacey trained her eyes on the interior of the shadow, but couldn't see the kitten.

She moved closer to the shadow. "Kitty?" she called tentatively. "Kitty, kitty!" She stared at the shadow on the pavement, looking hard into the dimness. She still didn't see the kitten, but she thought she saw movement within the shadow. And she heard something.

A plaintive meowing sound emanated from the depths of the shadow. The noise was faint, as though coming from far away. It suddenly became a high-pitched scream; then the there was silence.

Lacey heard a new sound, like sticks snapping. . . or like someone was crunching on pretzels.

Lacey began to fear that the kitten wasn't coming back.

She walked slowly toward the shadow, a slender little girl wearing white capris and a matching white shirt, her jet-black ponytail streaming down her back, crystal blue eyes wide with fear. The closer she came to the darkness, the colder she felt. A chill skittered down her spine and goosebumps broke out on her arms. She wrinkled her nose at the garbagy, rancid smell that floated up from the shadow.

Trembling just a little, Lacey stuck her sneakered foot toward it. The darkness seemed to swell. A finger of shadow snapped toward the toes of her right foot. She gasped when she felt contact, bringing with it a sensation of profound cold and the feeling of hot needles jabbing into her toes, all at the same time.

Lacey jumped back, feeling resistance as the shadow tried to wrap around her foot more securely. Her heartbeat sped up and sharp currents of fear lanced from her stomach into her chest. She yanked her foot away and broke contact with the shadow. She could almost sense disappointment and frustration coming from the black space.

THE SHADY SIDE

She backed away until she felt safe enough to turn her back on the shadow. Then she ran.

* * *

Lacey didn't tell her mom and dad about the shadow. She didn't think they would believe her. They never believed her about anything. Even when she tried to tell them about her brother, Lucas.

She didn't tell Lucas, either. He never listened to her. No matter what she said, he made fun of her. And then there was the other stuff he did. Lacey did her best to stay away from him.

Lucas hugged her too much. He touched her in places that felt wrong. He looked at her in a weird way that made her feel squirmy.

He had come to her room at night a couple of times, and she had screamed and screamed. But when her parents came, Lucas tricked them by telling them she was screaming from nightmares and he was just checking on her.

They didn't believe her.

That's why she always played at Holly's after school, even though she didn't like Holly all that much. Sometimes she went to Heather's. If she couldn't play at Holly's or Heather's she went to the library. If the library was closed, she went to the toy store on Main Street.

Anything not to be home alone with her brother.

She kept the shadow to herself, but she couldn't forget it. The hot-needle sensation in her toes faded after a while, leaving a cold numbness that stayed for the rest of her life.

* * *

That night, after she made her parents escort her up the stairs and check beneath her bed, in the closet, and behind her chair and window curtains, she shoved a book beneath the edge of her door so that it couldn't be opened, like she did every night. Her parents wouldn't let her have a lock on her door, but she had to protect herself, somehow.

She lay in her bed and thought about the shadow. It scared her. The smell, the sounds of the kitten that disappeared.

She thought that the shadow was like Lucas. There was something really wrong with him, something their parents couldn't see. He was a person, and the shadow was a shadow, but in the end, the two were both monsters.

* * *

Lacey avoided the Bric-A-Brac building for a couple of days, but it wasn't long before her curiosity drew her back to the parking lot.

The shadow was still there, despite the fact that the Saturday morning sunshine beamed down from the opposite direction than the day Lacey had discovered it. The first time she had seen the shadow, it had seemed natural because it was late in the day and the shadow lay beneath the Bric-A-Brac building, behind which the evening sun had been sinking.

But now, there was no reason for the shadow to be there. Maybe it wasn't a shadow, after all. Maybe it was really an old stain from a leaky car. But she thought the shadow was too big to be an oil stain. It was bigger than her. And it was shaped kind of like a person.

Lacey stood back at a safe distance and chewed a fingernail while she contemplated the shadow. It looked bigger than the first time she had seen it.

She decided to watch it for a while.

She found a sunny patch of grass next to the big brick building and sat down cross-legged. She stared at the shadow for a few minutes, trying not to blink. If something happened, she didn't want to miss it.

THE SHADY SIDE

After a few minutes, Lacey decided that she was enjoying herself, just sitting there in the sun on a summer Saturday morning. The breeze was slight; the broad expanse of the parking lot, still and quiet. She closed her eyes and inhaled deeply. Away from the heavy downtown traffic and away from the shadow, the air was clean and held just a hint of morning crispness that would soon give way to the yellow and green smells of sunshine and grass.

For the first time in a very, very long time, Lacey felt at peace. No hiding from Lucas. No kowtowing to Holly. Just sitting with the shadow.

Just being.

After a while, feeling stiff, she stood and stretched. Nothing was happening. The shadow was just a shadow, or an old stain, or whatever it was. She was almost disappointed.

She was about to turn to leave when movement caught her eye. A squirrel was running along a branch that belonged to a tree that stood just on the other side of the chain link fence. The squirrel chucked and twittered, flicking its tail at a second squirrel that ran along behind it.

The first squirrel dropped to the grass close to Lacey, and the second squirrel followed. She watched as they gamboled and played. They ran off the grass onto the pavement. Lacey held her breath as they neared the shadow. Both of the squirrels ran into the dark space – and promptly disappeared.

Lacey walked slowly toward the dark spot and halted a few steps away. Her nose wrinkled as the stench assailed her olfactory senses. She heard screeching sounds, then silence – then crunching noises, just like before, on the day of the kitten.

When the crunching noises stopped, there was silence. Lacey felt a strange sense that the shadow was sniffing the air; and then felt sure that the shadow had turned toward her, was looking at her.

But how could that be? It was just a big black spot in a parking lot. No eyes. No nose, no face.

But it *was* shaped like a person.

And she felt positive that it knew she was there.

And it had just eaten two squirrels. Three days before, it had eaten a kitten. Maybe it had eaten other things in the time it had been lying on the parking lot pavement. And how long had it actually been there?

The pleasant morning sunlight dimmed a little.

The shadow seemed to grow larger, to pulse. Lacey thought she could almost hear a deep *thrum* sound coming from it. And it was *rippling*, like the surface of a pond would ripple beneath the wind.

As she watched, part of the black space elongated and stretched toward her like an outstretched arm.

She snapped out of her daze and backed off until it was safe to turn and flee.

* * *

"*No way!* That's crazy!" Lacey held her Sweet Polly doll defensively. She should have known better than to bring her new doll to Holly's house.

"My birthday is tomorrow, and Sweet Polly rhymes with Sweet Holly," Holly said self-importantly, "So she really should be mine. You should give her to me as a birthday present."

"That's *stupid!* Why would I do that? Sweet Polly was a present to *me* from *my mom*. You can't have her!"

"Well then, maybe I won't let you play at my house anymore!"

"*Really?* Oh my *God!*"

"*Yeah!*"

This was the last straw. Lacey couldn't believe that Holly was going to try to take her brand-new doll from her. Her face red with anger, she prepared to stomp out of Holly's bedroom – but then she turned around.

"Okay," Lacey said sweetly. "I'll make a deal with you. You can have Sweet Polly, but only if we play what *I* want to play, next. Once we play the game that I want to play, then I'll give you Sweet Polly."

Holly considered this for a second, scrunching up her brown eyes in thought. "Okay," she said. "It's a deal."

Lacey smiled. "It's too nice outside to stay stuck in here, playing with dolls. Let's go outside. I know an awesome place to draw sidewalk pictures. No cars go there, because the gate is chained shut. You can bring your sidewalk chalk, and you get to pick all the best colors."

"Okay. Let me get my summer hat. My mom says I have to wear it, or my fair skin will burn."

Oh, please, Lacey thought. Her own skin was much lighter than Holly's, and *she* didn't need a stupid summer hat. But she smiled nicely as Holly crammed the straw hat down onto her platinum blonde hair.

Outside, Lacey said, "This way," and led Holly to the Bric-A-Brac parking lot.

After squeezing between the chained and padlocked gate, Holly said, "Wow, are you sure?" she gazed at the intimidating brick building, noting the broken windows and sensing the lonely air that surrounded it.

"I play here all the time, and I use it as a shortcut. It's perfectly safe. No one ever comes here and there's no traffic." Lacey picked a spot away from the shadow, but still in its vicinity. "This is a great spot!"

For once, Holly agreed with her. "I'm going to draw a boat on the ocean!"

"*I'm* drawing a garden with flowers!" Lacey laid Sweet Polly down in the nearby grass.

"That's a better idea. That's what *I'm* going to draw, instead of a boat!"

Lacey sighed, but didn't argue.

They spent a good part of the afternoon coloring on the blank canvas of the parking lot. When they were finished, that corner of the pavement was filled with pictures of flowers, trees, grass, sunshine, ocean, boats, bunnies, cats, butterflies, and stick-figure representations of family members.

Holly finally stood up and surveyed their work. She smiled, satisfied. "This is the best game we ever played. We should come back and do some more! But I have to go home, now." She held out her hand. "Sweet Polly, like you said in our deal."

Lacey, in anticipation of Holly's demand, was prepared. "Okay," she said. "But there's just one last part of the game we need to play. It will only take a minute, then you can have Sweet Polly and we can go."

Holly looked at her, hand on hip. Lacey had picked a good game this afternoon, so she was willing to listen. "Okay. What's the game?"

"It's a bet." Lacey indicated the shadow on the pavement. "I bet I can jump a bigger distance across that shadow than you can."

"Really? That's simple. I want to go first!"

Lacey smiled. "Of course you can, Holly." She held up Sweet Polly. "And when you're done jumping, she's yours."

Holly smiled back. She turned and looked at the shadow, then took a running start. At the edge of the shadow, she leaped. Her smile turned to a look of confusion as part of the darkness whipped up and wrapped around her leg, snatching her out of the air. Her summer hat fell into the darkness and disappeared as she struggled to crawl across the pavement and sank into it, instead.

"*Lacey!*" Holly screamed, twisting her neck, trying to look at her friend. "*Help me!*"

THE SHADY SIDE

Lacey shouted, "You *can't have* Sweet Polly! And you're a sucky friend!" She turned her back on Holly's pleas and screams, which quickly fell silent. This time, the crunching noises were really loud, snapping and echoing against the building, across the empty parking lot.

After slipping between the chained gates, Lacey skipped home, clutching Sweet Polly tightly in her arms.

She was sure that Lucas would love to come and see her pretty chalk pictures.

HELENA

The percussion of thunder shakes the house. A few seconds later, torrents of rain slam down onto the roof.

Helena looks toward the picture window in the living room. The rain pummels leaves and small branches from her cherry trees in the front yard.

She winces as she places one slippered foot in front of the other while she makes her tedious way to the old chair beside the window. The excess weight that she has borne for over thirty years has weakened her ankles and hips. Walking is painful for her, but it has been so long since it rained that Helena welcomes the storm and wants to watch it pass by.

Helena sees her reflection in the darkened glass of the window as she moves around the old oak dining room table. The image is distorted: a large, round figure, dressed in a white terry housecoat over loose polyester clothing. The head is fringed in thin, gray, wispy hairs. The jowls droop, dragging the corners of the mouth down in a perpetual frown.

She lowers herself into the old chair with a sigh of relief. This chair is Helena's friend. Originally owned by her great-grandmother, the chair is not just an antique: it is a centenarian, and shows it in the faded, threadbare gold and orange silk upholstered seat and in the sturdy dark wood of its once ornately carved arms. The carvings are now worn almost smooth, like stones at the bottom of a riverbed.

Over the years the chair's seat and back have taken Helena's shape and are perfectly tailored to fit her body. In this chair, she has rested and watched the soft and gentle snows fall, year after year. She has watched the crisp red and yellow leaves blow about in miniature tornadoes, harried by the autumn winds. She has witnessed the blossoming of the cherry trees, whose seeds she planted with her own hands. Sitting in this chair, Helena has experienced the pastel beauty of countless gold, red, orange, and pink sunrises and sunsets.

Today she sits alone in the gloomy house. She hasn't turned on any lights. She hasn't used them in three weeks.

The rain smashes Helena's white cherry blossoms to the ground, where the hard spikes of water soon churn them to tiny pieces in the new mud. A strange mixture of amber and yellow-green tints the sky.

Beauty in all its savage fury, Helena thinks; tears roll down her pasty white cheeks.

She has waited in this house alone for nearly half a decade, unsure of exactly what it is she waits for. Death, maybe. The one thing she *is* sure of is that at the age of seventy-six, with her body crippled in several different ways, she is ready to go.

Her five children flew from the nest years ago. Kurt, the oldest, chose his own way out at the age of thirty-eight. Less than three months after Kurt's wife Lorraine had a miscarriage and lost what would have been their first child, she had left Kurt. Shortly after Lorraine's desertion, Kurt hooked a hose to his car's exhaust pipe and snaked it through the rear passenger window. He sat in his driver's seat and waited while the car idled in the garage.

Helena's youngest daughter Chrissie escaped to Europe three years after Kurt's death. Helena hasn't heard from Chrissie since December of the year before last.

Katie and Mina are both married and settled down with their husbands and children. Katie is now a Canadian citizen; Mina and her family relocated to the Midwest.

Paul was the youngest child. After Paul's birth, Helena's husband, Eugene, had deserted the increasingly crowded Howell ship.

Paul died in Utica, New York. One sleepless night, he went out for a walk. He turned the corner of a building just in time to witness a man savagely beating a woman in a parking lot. Paul rushed to aid the woman, but her attacker turned on him, beating Paul so badly that he died in the hospital less than twenty-four hours later. Because of his intervention, the woman had survived.

Now, as thunder reverberates through her house and

THE SHADY SIDE

lightning forks the sky, Helena's grief racks her body. Her jowls and her flaccid arms shake as she sobs convulsively. The force of her sorrow seems to reflect the ruthlessness of the storm outside.

She tries to remember the last time she laughed, or even smiled, but nothing comes. She can't remember what it feels like to be happy and full of love, for family or for life. She is as empty a shell as her house is.

And she is exhausted.

She drags herself out of bed each morning and forces herself to bathe, to dress herself, to eat; and wonders why she even bothers. But the answer always comes automatically: to let go of the basic routine of life would be to give up – and giving up is wrong.

Why shouldn't I give up? Why keep up the fight? The years ahead will be as lonely as the ones gone by. The girls could care less. The boys are both dead. Most of my friends are, too. No one would miss me; there is no one left to care.

But then Helena's conscience reprimands this thinking. *"Giving up" is not the way life is done. As long as you are alive, you will take care of what you have left.*

Tears sting her eyes and blur her vision as she gazes through the front window.

She remembers how, when she was a young mother, she kicked her shoes off and ran through the soft grass, playing tag with her children. They screamed and laughed when she pushed them, singly or in pairs, on the tire swing tied up to the maple tree; the tire swing that now beats against the tree trunk, blown by the merciless storm wind.

On summer days, the kids splashed around in the little play pool and doused one another with the hose. After dinner, when dusk fell, they caught fireflies in jars and played hide-and-seek until bed time.

But now the kids are all gone. Only the ghost of their laughter remains.

Helena barely hears the pounding on the front door above the noise of the storm and her own sobbing.

She hastily wipes her sodden face on the collar of her robe. Knowing that it will take her too long to reach the front door, and too tired to try, anyway, she calls out, "Come in!"

She hears the front door open and close, followed by the sound of shoes being wiped on the rug in front of it. Her body stiffens with apprehension. Who would be out visiting in weather like this?

He comes around the edge of the large open doorway from the foyer. Helena recognizes him, even in the shadowed gloom of the house. Her breath catches in her throat.

"*K-Kurt?*" she whispers.

"Hi, Momma!"

Helena's first-born child and first-dead son looks well, despite having been buried in the ground for so many years. He wears a red flannel shirt and denim dungarees that look brand new. And despite his arrival out of a rain storm, he is dry. And his face – well, his face – is *tan*.

His mouth tightens in concern as he walks toward her.

"Momma! What's wrong? You're crying!" he kneels

THE SHADY SIDE

beside her and takes her hand.

Helena stares at him. "Wh-what - where did you come from?"

"That doesn't matter, Momma. Not a bad place, though. You wouldn't believe it! I understand so much more now than I used to." He looks toward the doorway that leads into the foyer. "And I brought someone with me!"

Helena's face turns three shades paler.

"*Surprise*, Momma!"

The figure of her youngest son, Paul, emerges through the doorway.

"Uh, uh…"

"Oh, you don't have to say anything, Momma. I understand." Paul looks younger than Helena remembers, but he still wears his trademark crooked grin. And he is dry, like his big brother.

"B-but…" Helena looks at the floor. Neither of the boys has left any wet footprints or puddles on the shiny dark hardwood floor or on the living room rug.

She shrinks back into the safety of her chair.

Kurt smiles up at her with straight, white teeth. His hand is warm. "Momma, don't be afraid. Everything is okay. See? Look." He points out the front window. Helena, her eyes wide and her body trembling with fear, turns her head and looks.

The storm has dissipated. The sun shines in a high, blue sky. Helena's cherry trees have made it through the storm undamaged. She examines the trees more closely and thinks it odd that they seem to have more blossoms now than they did before the rain's brutal onslaught. The branches should be bare. And the burned-brown grass in the front yard, which should be a mud-churned mess, looks green, lush and soft.

"Wouldn't you like to walk out there, Momma? You should take off your slippers and come for a walk with me and Paul. How does that sound?"

"Uh," Helena hears herself stammer, "I don't move so well, these days." She is still trying to overcome her shock at seeing her deceased sons walking around in her living room. How could she go out for a stroll with not just one, but *two*, dead men?

I must be seeing things. I've gotten so old; or maybe I'm crazy, or maybe there really is a devil, and he's here to trick me out of my soul.

"*No*, Momma," Paul says. He moves to stand beside her and grins that silly, crooked grin. "You're perfectly sane. You know exactly who we are and that we aren't here to hurt you. We've really missed you."

Helena looks into his dark brown eyes. *Was I talking out loud?*

"And another thing," he continues, "Why must people always associate the dead with evil?"

Silence reigns for a moment. Then the tick-tick-tick of the old cuckoo clock comes into the foreground of Helena's consciousness. She looks out the window again.

She sees children, her own boys and girls. They run about the yard playing tag, laughing and shrieking, while the tire swing creaks back and forth from the old maple. Cherry blossoms fly past like snowflakes, borne by a late summer wind.

This can't be real, Helena thinks.

THE SHADY SIDE

"Come on, we'll show you!" Paul looks like an excited puppy, ready to go for a romp in the park.

"I think you should come with us, Momma," Kurt says. "It may not be as bad as you think."

He stands, takes Helena's hand, and attempts to pull her out of her old chair. Paul grabs her other hand and helps Kurt pull. Helena shifts, preparing to work her great bulk out of its resting place. To her surprise she stands easily, nearly falling forward onto her face because she overcompensates as she tries to balance her weight. Bewildered, she looks out the window again and catches her own reflection in the glass.

Gone is the obese woman with the stretched-out abdomen and loose jowls. Before Helena stands the image of a slim, young woman. Her face is slender and pretty, the skin still firm. Her hair is dark and long. The blanket-like terrycloth housecoat and the polyester pantsuit have been replaced by an ankle-length picnic dress with a full, cornflower colored skirt and short, puffy white sleeves.

Kurt puts his hands on Helena's shoulders and gently turns her to face him. "See? That's who you really are. That's who you have always been, to me."

"No," Paul says. "She doesn't look like that. This is what she looks like." He points to the window.

There is the young woman again, this time dressed in shorts and one of her husband's oversized shirts. Her hair is pulled back in a ponytail. Lines and dark circles are just beginning to form around her eyes.

Kurt sighs. "Does it really matter, Paul? She's beautiful, anyway."

"Oh, sure," Paul retorts, "How come when I do something *my* way instead of yours, it doesn't matter?"

The ghost of a smile plays on Helena's lips, and some of the tension eases away from her shoulders. These are definitely her sons, squabbling in their old familiar way.

"Do we have to stand here and argue on this day, of all days? Can't we show a little respect for our mother by not fighting?"

Stung, Paul crosses his arms in front of his chest and sulks.

"Now, if we can get back to what we were doing," Kurt says. "Let's go, Momma. Don't think. Just *do*. Trust me." Kurt takes Helena's hand and leads her to the front door. She moves without wheezing or any kind of physical pain. With the release of the extra weight, Helena feels as though she is floating, like a helium balloon in a lazy breeze.

Kurt pulls the door open and sweeps his arm forward, gesturing her ahead. "How long has it been since you've taken a walk outside?"

Helena looks outside and hesitates.

A gentle spring breeze touches her face, warmed by the sunshine. Birds flit to and fro and settle in the hedge by the road, chirping. Butterflies flutter about in their aimless-looking way, and the insects buzz in chorus.

Have I gone insane?

"Momma." Kurt's voice commands her to turn and face him. "You need to let it go." He looks at her intently. "You know it, we know it, and God knows it. You know why we're here."

Paul steps up behind Kurt and looks at her over

Kurt's shoulder. "I love you, Momma." His affection for her shows in his eyes.

Helena sighs and rolls her eyes. *What the hell. Do I really have anything better to do?*

She kicks off her slippers, now three sizes too big for her shapely young feet, and steps through the door onto the front porch. The wood feels smooth and warm.

A surge of excitement drives back her fear and suspicion.

Kurt follows her out of the house, then Paul, who closes the door behind him. They come to stand on either side of their mother, both offering her their elbows. She entwines her arms through those of her two sons, and the three of them descend the old wooden steps of her lifelong home.

Helena closes her eyes in the warm yellow sunshine as the soft, cool grass cushions her bare feet.

DEFENSIVE DRIVING

When Kaho Ali walked into the office, Sam nearly pissed his pants. The bearded man was pure mass, monstrously huge. Each of his thundering footsteps shook the floor so that Sam could feel the vibrations travel through the soles of his shoes up through his legs.

"Samuel *Doo-dag*," said the bear of a man, holding Sam's referral page before him. He lowered the page just enough for him to look over the top edge at Sam, his dark, almond-shaped eyes magnified behind the thick lenses of his glasses. "*Doo-dagh?*"

Sam cleared his throat nervously. "*Du*-dah. The "g" is silent." He focused on the nameplate on the man's desk. The white block letters etched against the black background spelled out the man's name: "*Kaho Ali*".

"Well, you can call me Kaho. We can dispense with the *Mr.*" He leafed through the rest of the pages of Sam's record. "With a last name pronounced *Doo-dah*, no wonder you're having problems. How did you get through school?" He shook his head. "*Tsk, tsk*. A "g" doesn't exist if it's silent." He looked over the page again. Sam tried not to squirm beneath the steady gaze.

THE SHADY SIDE

"Why the road rage? That's all you have on your record. No drugs, alcohol, no thieving. All of your crimes are vehicular. What's going on?"

Sam exhaled and ran a hand across his blonde-brown buzz cut. "I get behind the wheel and start driving, and people are assholes. They're rude and ignorant of the rules of the road. They do stupid things." He shrugged helplessly. "I get pissed. Just so angry, I can't help it."

Kaho the giant set the papers down on his desk and straightened his floral button-down Hawaiian shirt before leaning back in his chair. His hands rested in his lap, fingers loosely interlaced.

He contemplated the gangly, scruffy man. His paperwork put him at twenty-eight years old, but he looked easily ten years older. His face was creased with worry lines, and a deep vertical frown line had formed between his watery blue eyes. His clothes were shabby and worn, but clean, as was the man, himself. His nails were bitten down to the quick.

Kaho leaned forward, his tan face earnest beneath his thick, black beard. He reminded Sam of Paul Bunyan; only, a Hawaiian version.

"I don't know what happened to you," Kaho said. "I don't know whether you were beaten by your dad or bullied in school. Frankly, I don't see why the judge bothered with this instead of sending you straight to the pen. Maybe he thought that remanding you to my care would be the fastest way to positive results. He gave you a real chance here, you know? You could be sitting your ass in prison. You know that, right?"

Sam looked down at his hands, his palms sweating against his blue jeans. He nodded.

"You started with tickets, points, suspensions. Revocation. Reinstatement. Conditional. But now you've been to jail three times. Three months, six months, a year. Each time is longer than the last. And you aren't afraid of going to prison? And what's more, don't you realize that when you lose it on the road, you become one of those 'assholes' you were just talking about?"

Sam sat still. Out of The Beast, he was meek and humble.

Christened The Beast by Sam's father, Phillip Michael Dudagh, the 1989 Chevy Silverado 1500 was Sam's best friend. They had both been born the same year. Phillip Dudagh had lovingly maintained the truck, which Sam had inherited upon his father's death. The Beast was the only item that remained of his early life with his parents.

The Beast was more than just a truck to Sam: it had served as his ride and his home, on different occasions. He had taken up the care and feeding of The Beast just as his father had taught him before he passed away, and the Silverado was always there for Sam to rely on when all else was gone.

Kaho sat back again. "Sam. Look at me." Sam looked at him. "I think I can see what's going on here." He opened up a bottom drawer of his desk. He set an object on his desk. "This is Ualani. Isn't she beautiful? I carved and assembled her myself."

Sam stared at the miniature hula dancer, his expression confused. "I don't understand."

"No, of course you don't." Kaho smiled, his teeth gleaming whitely against the bristly black frame of his beard. "Let me explain." He nudged the figure with his finger. The slight touch set her in motion, her upper body bobbling gently. "Go ahead. You can pick her up. Look at her. Notice all of her details, and how she feels as you hold her in your hand."

Still not understanding, Sam reached out haltingly and touched the hula dancer's bare foot, whose tiny toenails were painted light pink. He gently picked her up. She was lighter than he thought she would be.

THE SHADY SIDE

Ualani's fingernails were painted the same delicate pink as her toenails. Her face was natural, without any sign of makeup around her chocolate-brown eyes, no added color upon her smiling lips.

A wreath of aromatic white orchids encircled her head, and thick tresses of surprisingly soft and life-like hair spilled from beneath it. A leis of white orchids also hung from around her neck, falling over her chest and then curving over her teeny smooth wooden breasts, which were clad in a light pink strapless bikini top. Her lower abdomen curved outward in a small bulge above the authentic grass skirt. Sam ran a finger down the calf of one of the smooth brown legs and flinched when, for a second, he thought the skin felt warm to his touch and had the give and softness of real human skin.

He looked at the dancer's face and nearly fumbled her when one of her eyelids dropped in a quick wink. Then her face was still again in its perpetual smile.

Sam blinked. Did he imagine that wink? He looked up at Kaho questioningly.

"She's beautiful, isn't she?" Kaho asked.

Sam nodded. "Yes, you do really good work. But I still don't get why you're showing her to me."

Kaho removed his glasses and rubbed his face. "Do you see how you are handling her?"

Sam looked at the dancer in his hands, then quickly stood her back on Kaho's desk, careful not to let her fall.

"You are being gentle with her. You are treating her kindly. This is the change you need to make when you are in your vehicle and you begin feeling angry with your fellow travelers. And now, Ualani will be your traveling companion." Kaho stood, towering over Sam, who stared in awe at the mountainous man. Once again, the man's stature reminded Sam of the legendary Paul Bunyan, except he was pretty sure Paul Bunyan had never worn cargo shorts and Jesus sneakers during a harsh Northeastern winter.

Sam nearly cowered when Kaho came around the end of the desk, dwarfing him. The giant dropped a huge brown hand on Sam's shoulder – and Sam's anxiety dissipated like mist in a strong wind. He relaxed against the back of his chair.

"Son, I believe that the stress of your past has become baggage that you haven't been able to lose through counseling and discipline. You don't care about yourself enough to be afraid of prison, since being incarcerated didn't faze you. You've injured three people, destroyed private and public property, and put your own life into jeopardy. Are you married?"

Sam shook his head. "No."

"Children? A girlfriend? A *pet?*"

Sam shook his head again.

"Yet you have a long roster of loyal family and friends who vouch for your character, as well as your even temper. It's like you've got a monster alter-ego hidden inside that surfaces when dealing with the anxiety of traveling on the road with other people. I see a lonely man who has never experienced real companionship, and maybe has never received love, compassion, or understanding, or if he has experienced these things, they must have gone wrong somehow; and therefore does not know how to bestow these gifts upon others.

"So what you are going to do, beginning today, is put Ualani on your dashboard. She will travel with you wherever you go. Your goal is to keep her standing and dancing her graceful dance. If she slides, if she falls onto the floor, if she hits the windshield due to any of your angry outbursts while your vehicle is in motion, she alone will be your judge and jury, and she will enforce whatever sentence she sees fit."

THE SHADY SIDE

Sam sat still for a moment, staring at Ualani. This man must be crazy. "Um – not to be disrespectful -"

"Kaho," said Kaho.

Sam cleared his throat. "Kaho," he affirmed, "But Ualani is a doll?"

Kaho clapped him on the shoulder and turned to resume his seat. "She *does* look like a doll, doesn't she? But she is a *dancer*. I can't explain her benefits to you, son. But you will soon see. What you need to learn is that those other people on the road? They are just *people*, Sam. They are human. Yes, some of them drive like idiots. You are not the only driver that has ever felt enraged at the oblivious attitudes of others with whom you must share the road. But think about this: Have you ever made a mistake, a genuine *mistake*, while you were driving? No, not hitting someone or running over someone's fence. An *innocent* mistake."

Sam's face reddened. "Yes."

"And what would you ask of the others around you when you make a simple, innocent mistake?"

"Um... forgiveness? Understanding?"

Sam jumped in his chair when the big man clapped his hands, delighted. "*Precisely!*" Then the smile dropped from Kaho's face. "The lesson that you have *not* learned through your previous experiences is that you need to demonstrate compassion, understanding, and forgiveness with your fellow man. We reap the consequences of our actions. This is your final opportunity to learn. If you don't, there's nothing I can do for you."

"But isn't this defensive driving? I thought it was a course. I don't have to come in and attend class?"

"You've already done the standard defensive driving courses. More than once. It isn't your knowledge that is lacking. It is your *soul*. Your vehicle will be your classroom, hands-on. Ualani will be your teacher." Kaho tipped his head back and looked at the ceiling. "And Heaven help you if you don't learn this lesson."

Sam sat quietly for a moment, then ventured a question: "So what do I – how do I-"

"Please don't tell me that you've never seen a hula dancer in a car before."

"Um, sorry. I haven't."

Kaho sighed. "Whatever happened to those days? Like I said, you put her on your dashboard. It's about balance, Samuel. Ualani's torso and lower body have each been painstakingly carved in two separate pieces. Her upper body balances on her waist. Applied external force causes her upper body to move, creating Ualani's own personal hula dance. You need to drive carefully in order to keep Ualani balanced. Don't let her slide around, and don't let her fall and break apart. She will be your mood minder, your conscience."

Sam shook his head. "But she's so *light!* She barely weighs as much as a piece of paper. There are no weights on her feet or legs to keep her in one place."

The big man smiled and reached in the drawer again. He handed Sam a flat piece of black plastic with two raised, curved openings. "Therein lies the challenge, Samuel. This base is all I can give you. Her feet fit into these little spaces. Other than that, it is up to you to keep her in place. Take her now and go about your business." He neatened Sam's papers and placed them in a manila file folder.

Sam stared at Kaho Ali.

The man looked up at him. "Good day, Samuel *Doo-dah*. And good luck."

"Don't I have to report back?"

"No. From here on in, you are under Ualani's supervision."

As Sam exited Kaho's office, he caught the big man singing under his breath, *"All de doodah-fucking-day..."*

THE SHADY SIDE

Sam rolled his eyes. It wasn't like he'd never heard that one before.

* * *

Sam inserted Ualani's tiny feet into the spaces on the plastic base and set her down on the center of the Silverado's dashboard. She stood facing him, her arms bent at the elbows, delicate fingers gracefully extended, poised to begin her dance at any time. Sam examined her nut-brown face, her dark eyes looking at him, smiling happily. He could smell the lush scent of the orchids encircling her head and neck.

Her gracious smile offered no answers, and Sam was beginning to think he had hallucinated her wink. He reached out and turned her so that she was facing the windshield and he could only see the sweep of her black hair.

He felt like he had suddenly been tossed into an episode of *The Twilight Zone*. It made no sense to him that Kaho Ali had simply handed a bobbling hula dancer to put on his dashboard and sent him on his merry way.

There had to be something *more*. Classes, counseling, community service. *Something.*

Didn't there?

He shrugged to himself. There was no reason to look a gift horse in the mouth. It was the judge's decision to send him to the giant Hawaiian. And Kaho Ali was right. He had done all of the counseling. He had done anger management. He had attended defensive driving courses. None of it had helped to keep him calm in a moving vehicle. End of story.

He started The Beast and backed out of the parking space.

Ualani's body undulated slightly.

He wasn't supposed to let her slide or fall. *Why?* He just didn't get it.

Still, there was something about the delicate hula dancer that made him more mindful as he drove home. He took the corners carefully and kept his foot light on the gas pedal so that he could ease down on the brakes when he approached stop signs and red lights.

Once, he pushed the gas pedal a little too hard and The Beast jumped forward. Ualani slid backward toward the edge of the dashboard. Sam reached out and snatched her up in his hand before she fell. He replaced her in her spot in the center of the dashboard. Afterward, he was more careful, and Ualani bobbled gently on his dashboard all the way home, where both she and Sam arrived without incident.

After he had exited the truck, he turned around and looked at Ualani through the windshield. Her hand was extended, making it look like she was waving.

He lifted his hand in return.

* * *

The sun beams down from a clear blue sky, warming Sam's face. An occasional wisp of cloud stretches itself above, and a warm breeze carries the scent of fresh orchids to him. He inhales deeply.

He is aware that he is dreaming.

He looks out to the ocean. A giant man stands far out in the waves. He resembles Kaho Ali, except that this man is gargantuan. Kaho looks like a midget compared to him, and he makes Sam feel as small as an ant.

He looks down the beach and there is Ualani, walking across the sand toward him. She is barefoot and is dressed exactly the way she was when he placed her on his dashboard earlier that day: Grass skirt, light pink bikini top, and white orchid leis and wreath encircling her neck and head. Her thick black tresses stream back behind her in the warm breeze.

THE SHADY SIDE

She smiles as she walks toward him. Her white teeth stand out in contrast to her brown skin. Sam realizes that when she is a doll, Ualani's white teeth are hidden behind her closed, smiling lips.

His heart begins to race as he watches the woman approach. He has never seen a more beautiful woman in his life. The very sight of her grows a bruised ache within his chest and a painful tightening in his shorts. He glances down and sees that he is, indeed, wearing shorts, not the pajama bottoms he had tossed on before slipping between his sheets.

Is it really him that she is smiling at? He turns and looks behind him, and the empty beach stretches far into the distance, bordered on the left by pale blue water and overhead by deep blue sky.

He turns back to face Ualani and notices how hot the white sand feels on the soles of his feet and between his toes. Every breath he takes is loud, echoing in his ears.

Ualani stops in front of him. She inclines her head slightly to the side and takes his hand. Hers is small and warm. She leans forward and kisses the corner of his mouth; her lips are soft, full and warm. He closes his eyes.

* * *

Sam woke to pale, weak winter sunlight intruding into his bedroom around his partially pulled curtains.

"Nooo," he groaned, pulling the blanket up over his head. He snuggled into the warm cave he had created. "Five minutes," he mumbled.

But he was awake now. He sighed. Knowing he couldn't fight the inevitable, he threw the covers off. He sat up and rubbed his eyes, then turned sideways and put his bare feet to the hardwood floor beside his bed.

Cold. And grainy?

He looked down, his vision still a little sleep-blurred, and saw the white grains of sand that had fallen from his feet on to the scratched hardwood. There were more particles stuck to the sides of his feet. He lifted one foot. Sure enough, there was a sparse layer of sand stuck to the skin on the bottom.

"What the?" Puzzled, Sam yanked the top sheet and blankets all the way down to the foot of his bed.

The sand was only slightly darker than the worn white sheets, but there was plenty of it peppered between them at the bottom of the bed. An image of the idyllic beach in his dream drifted briefly across his mind's eye - and Ualani. Her kiss.

Damn, he needed to take care of some morning business.

He shivered and remembered where he was. *This is not a beach on some island. This is winter in upstate New York.*

His feet were cold. He needed slippers. A robe. More blankets. Sweaters, long johns. Things to keep him warm in this frozen hellscape of a winter.

He didn't make much cash at his job as a mechanic assistant and he was still paying fines, court surcharges, and restitution for his vehicular crimes. He rented a crappy little studio apartment to save money. All of the utilities were included, which sucked, because his heat was controlled by the stingy landlord, who didn't want to pay out to keep his tenants warm.

Old and worn. Hand-me-down. That described all of the furnishings that had come with Samuel Dudagh's apartment. The coffee table was scratched and scarred from hard use, and it looked like a beaver had chewed the legs. The orange, weird-textured upholstering of the sagging sofa was threadbare; a portion of one of its foam cushions pushed through a large tear in the fabric of the cushion cover.

THE SHADY SIDE

His two towels were nearly as thin as tissue paper and frayed and the edges. Both of them together barely contained enough material to dry him off after his shower. Shivering in the chilly air, Sam pulled on a stained but clean sweatshirt and pair of jeans.

Maybe he should get rid of The Beast. That would decrease all of his financial obligations. No paying for gas, insurance, oil changes. He didn't owe anything on the old thing; it was probably in the best shape of anything he actually owned. But if he gave up the Silverado, he would have to screw around finding a ride. And he worked forty minutes away, in the next county.

He shook his head. *What the fuck am I thinking? I can't give up The Beast. She's saved my ass more times than I can count.*

If there was only one thing he could count on, it was the Silverado. Having working wheels was important if you had no home, because you could drive to out-of-the-way places where you could spend the night undisturbed by lights, traffic, and cops knocking on your windows. As long as you had some gas, a sleeping bag and lots of extra blankets, you could stay warm and out of the cold. And use the AC and stay out of the sun, or set up the truck bed as a bed in a rural field beneath the stars and Milky Way on a summer night. And if work was short in one town, you could easily look for a job in the next one - long as you had working wheels.

Even during his stints in jail, Sam had made sure The Beast was taken care of. His Uncle Mitchell had taken her in and kept her safe when Sam was incarcerated. He said he didn't do it for Sam; he did it for his late brother Phillip, God rest his soul; even though the knowledge that the Silverado was the only thing of value Sam possessed in the world was an underlying factor to his uncle's kindness. He had also helped Sam save her from the Impound.

Whatever happened to Sam, wherever he went, he knew his dad's pickup truck would always be waiting for him when he returned. To this day, he kept everything he needed to survive in his truck bed: his tool box, sleeping bag and extra blankets, emergency kit, a small supply of dried food and Sterno, paper kitchen supplies, extra clothing, among other things. Collectively, the whole lot took up less than a quarter of the room in the truck bed. It all fit in the box.

By his own assessment, Sam shouldn't even be driving. He had been toeing the line long enough so that the courts had reinstated his driving privileges. Conditionally. But Sam knew his own limitations, and he feared it wouldn't be long before he screwed up again.

He brushed the sand from his feet and got moving.

He threw on his clothes, made a cup of instant coffee and buttered a single slice of bread for breakfast before donning his boots. Seeing the sole of his right boot flapping loosely, he remembered how his feet had been soaked and freezing at work the day before.

Rummaging around in a kitchen junk drawer, he found some duct tape and wrapped it around his boot, secured the loose sole, and added extra tape at the seam to prevent further leaks.

He brushed his teeth and looked at his face in the mirror. Damn, but he was looking old. And tired. He shouldn't look - or feel - this tired, as young as he was.

He was in a lot of trouble. He wondered if it wouldn't just be worth it to violate again and let them send him to prison. Meals and board provided. Would it be worse than this?

He grabbed his coat, pulled an old knit cap down over his exposed ears, and headed outside to start the truck and let it thaw for a few minutes.

The cold immediately enveloped Sam's body through his coat and jeans. His breath plumed out in foggy clouds, and his boots crunched on the top frozen surface crust of snow.

The Beast's windows had iced over the previous night. He hoped the ice wasn't too thick and would thaw quickly. He held his breath as he turned the key in the driver side door lock and let it out, relieved, when the door opened easily. He slid into the seat, pumped the gas pedal once and turned the key. The engine turned over and The Beast roared to life, then quieted to idle. He turned the heat switch to its highest setting and turned the windshield wipers on just to see how long he would need to let The Beast run.

As he watched the windshield, Sam saw Ualani standing on his dashboard. A small smile played on his lips. "Hey, Tiny Dancer! I forgot about you," he said, reaching for her. A brief memory of his dream flashed through his thoughts; then vanished just as quickly when he noticed that Ualani was standing facing toward The Beast's interior – toward *him*. And he remembered exiting The Beast the day before and turning to look at the hula dancer through the windshield glass – and waving to her.

But here she stood, facing the truck's cab. Facing *him*. Sometime during the night, Ualani had turned around.

Or *been* turned around.

He quickly checked the glove box and the console. There was really nothing in the cab that was worth stealing. And why would anyone bother to break into The Beast and turn the doll around? He shook his head as he exited the Silverado.

Back in the living room, he finished his coffee and thought about Ualani and Kaho Ali. Yesterday's meeting with the defensive driving instructor now seemed far away and surreal. And Sam was beginning to have some ideas that maybe weren't so realistic.

He locked his apartment and went back to his truck. He regarded Ualani's smiling face briefly before reaching out and turning her to face the windshield.

"I'm sorry," he said. "I have enough problems with my driving. I know I'll get too nervous trying to drive with you looking at me."

The auto repair shop was already busy when Sam got there. A tall, hook-nosed man with a long face stood in the back corner, talking to Sam's co-workers. The man's head was topped with a shock of thick, unruly salt-and-pepper hair that seemed to have a life of its own. As he spoke, some of the wavy strands floated to and fro in an apparent draft that eddied around his head.

Sam found Tim Shepherd, his trainer. "Who's that?" Sam said, nodding his head in stranger's direction.

"That's Lamb," Tim said. "He's the owner. Name's Lawrence, but his nickname is Lamb, on account of how he's so laid back. He's a good boss. Don't worry, you're good, you've been doing fine," he assured Sam when he saw how nervous Sam looked.

Lamb approached the two men. "You the new hire?" he asked Sam, looking him up and down with friendly interest.

Sam nodded. "Yes, sir."

"What's your name again?"

"Sam Dudagh."

Lamb addressed Tim. "Where's Jessup?"

"Called in," Tim answered.

Lamb turned back to Sam. "Come on back to the office with me." He led the way to the back and held the door open for Sam.

"You been here how long?" Lamb asked, after they were seated.

Sam tried to concentrate on Lamb's face, instead of the hair that floated around Lamb's head as though being moved by underwater currents. "About a month and a half."

"I've read your resume, Sam. Says you're a certified auto tech. Diagnostics and engine repair, brakes and exhaust, et cetera, the core 8 for cars, plus secondary certs."

"Yes, sir."

"And experience. Four years. People really like you, you've got some excellent recommendations."

"Thank you, sir."

Lamb pushed papers around on his desk, then searched under receipt books, bills, and various pieces of mail. He found what he was looking for and handed Sam a piece of paper. "I'm giving you a raise and a promotion. Our Head Tech takes too much time off. He's undependable. Can't count on him. He's done. He's had two warnings, three strikes, he's out. Can I depend on you to speak no more about that?"

It took a second for Sam to catch up to what Lamb meant, then he nodded, even though he hadn't yet spoken a word about it.

"Read that form and sign it. It explains how much of a raise you're getting, that you are being promoted to Head Tech, and you are receiving a $300 sign-on bonus. You didn't get that yet, did you?"

Speechless, Sam shook his head.

"Your signature says you accept all three. I'll give you a manual that tells you what your duties are in your new position. Oh, and before I forget," Lamb bent down, rifling through his top desk drawer. "Now, where the hell did I put it? Here's one!" He dropped a white business card in front of Sam. "Go see that lady at that address. I can't have my Head Tech wearing duct-taped boots and a see-through jacket. I'll get a bad reputation. Jackie'll fix you up. Why you dressed like that?"

"Um, rent. Fines, restitution, and things."

"Hm. Who you renting from?"

"Adam Greenfield."

"Hell no, boy. He'll freeze you to death, and you'll never have any money for a life. I know for a fact he only does month-to-month. Tell Jackie I said she should see about a new place for you. You got fines, you're paying restitution, bring the paperwork to Jackie, and we'll pay off what you owe. Fly right here, and things will improve for you, in a hurry."

"Yes, sir. Thank you."

"No, sir. First name basis, son. You Sam, me Lamb." Lamb smiled. His teeth were big and gave Lamb's face a comical, horsey look. Sam smiled back, mesmerized by Lamb's strong features and hair still waving in the breeze that Sam couldn't feel.

"I'm giving you the day off to get your living arrangements in order and do some shopping. Come back tomorrow with a new jacket and warm boots. Stop and see Casey in her cubicle next door and pick up your sign-on bonus check. You already met her when you filled out your new employee paperwork, yes?"

Sam nodded.

Lamb stood, and Sam followed suit. "I don't know what to say – Lamb."

Lamb held out his hand. "Generosity toward others is good for the soul. I'm giving back what I've been given. I don't like to see others suffer. I have an idea how much you've suffered. I can see it in your face. If I don't give you a break, who else is gonna?"

Sam shook his hand. "Thank you."

"See you tomorrow."

Still speechless and not quite believing his sudden good fortune, Sam slid into his driver seat and started The Beast. He looked at Ualani.

She was turned facing him again. Her smile seemed somehow broader than it had, before.

THE SHADY SIDE

First Kaho Ali, now Lamb, both cutting him breaks. Sam touched the front edge of his knit cap in a brief gesture of acknowledgement. "Good luck smiles upon me, it seems, Tiny Dancer." he said. Instead of turning her around to face away from him, Sam left Ualani where she was, so that he could see her face as he drove home.

Ualani bobbled happily as Sam eased The Beast out of the parking lot.

* * *

Sam packed up his few meager belongings and moved into his new place that day. None of the bedding or the bed in his old place belonged to him. He left it as it was, not bothering to clean anything. The place was spotless. He didn't have much to clean.

He had forgotten about the sand on the floor and between his sheets at the foot of the bed.

The new place was furnished, as was the studio apartment he had vacated; however, the furniture in the new apartment was in good condition. There were no holes in the sofa's soft gray upholstery; the coffee table was sturdy and bore few signs of wear and tear, and there was a re-used hotel recliner that still worked. Sam's new place had a bedroom with adjoining bathroom and a kitchen that was separate from the living room.

And he controlled the heat.

He cranked it up to seventy-two and put away his new things. The old woman, Jackie, had provided him with a free coat and boots, both with tags still on, as well as a new package of socks. She'd loaded him down with sheets, blankets, towels, a set of dishes still in the box, cups, and utensils.

Despite his issues, Sam had always worked and paid his own way. Though grateful for Lamb's generosity, he felt guilty at accepting what amounted to enough household items to fill half of his pickup's bed, and he said as much to Jackie.

"The only thing you need to do to pay Lamb back is do well," Jackie told him. "And one day, you will be able to do the same for someone else. That's where all these things came from," she added. "Everything I just gave you came from others that Lamb helped. They paid back by donating, now that they can."

Sam counted his lucky stars for this; he was able to use his $300 bonus to buy groceries and other necessities.

By early evening, his place was set up. He didn't have much in the way of personal items, but he did have a lot of sketch books, charcoal and colored pencils. Jail had given Sam plenty of time to get into the habit of drawing every day. Comics, everyday scenes, portraits; he had several sketch books full of art.

He turned on the television that had been provided with the apartment and settled down on the sofa beneath the blanket with a notebook and charcoal pencil.

He started by sketching a caricature of Kaho Ali; first, as Sam had seen the man in his office, glasses and all; then as a giant, forty feet tall. He did the same with Ualani – first, as the bobbling dashboard dancer; then as a full-size living woman. Then he moved on to Lamb, sketching the comical horsey face and hair waving to and fro above his head.

As he sketched, he turned the events of the past two days over and over in his head. Throughout most of his life he had been in and out of trouble, and his checkered history had caused him nothing but hardship. People stopped trusting him as soon as they discovered his criminal record. No one had bothered cutting him a break – until now. And all of his recent good fortune seemed too good to be true.

Sam's doubts didn't prevent him from falling asleep as soon as his head hit the thick, fluffy pillow.

THE SHADY SIDE

* * *

Back on the beach again. Sam can smell the expanse of white hot-sand blended with the damp saltiness of the ocean and ripe green of the nearby hala trees that form a line between the beach and the woods. The deep blue of the sky, the dark blue of the ocean, the white beach, all of the colors seem to stand out brilliantly beneath the high summer sun, whose reflected light sparkles like rhinestones on the surface of the nearby shallows.

Sam feels nothing but heat: summer sun that burns his shoulders; the white-hot sand that burns the soles of his feet. He moves to the water's edge, where he seeks relief on the much cooler packed wet brown sand.

A loud "SMACK!" reverberates in from the ocean. Shortly thereafter, huge breakers roll into shore. Looking out between the mangroves that dot the surf, Sam sees Kaho Ali's massive silhouette splashing and stomping further out in the deep water. Kaho looks inland. Sam can't see the giant's expression against the bright, sunny backdrop, but Kaho lifts a hand in greeting. Sam raises his own in return.

A giant nose breaks the surface of the water beside Kaho as a sperm whale launches out of the water, leaping high into the air. As gargantuan as Kaho is, the whale has a good twenty feet on him and makes him look short.

The whale turns in the air. As it rotates, its fin meets Kaho's hand in a whale-human "high-five". The whale lands with a SMACK! Waves roll inland from its point of impact.

A feather light touch brushes Sam's shoulder. He turns, and there is Ualani, standing behind him. Her face is somber for just a second before it breaks into what is beginning to be a familiar smile that lights her face, beaming from her brown eyes. She takes Sam's hand and tugs him gently with her.

His eyes are fixed on her smooth shoulders as she leads him toward the tree line. His gaze travels down her arms, her back, to the grass skirt. Her movement is sinuous and seductive.

The lush, sweet smell of her orchid leis drifts back to him. It is a cool, feminine scent, and even in the heat the smell makes the hair on the nape of his neck stand up and he shivers with a sudden chill; it is as though a cloud has crossed the sun. Then the chill is gone and the heat returns.

They reach the tree line, where the shade provides relief from the high, direct sunlight. A white hammock appears, stretched loosely between two trees. Ualani dips her head briefly and gestures to it with graceful fingers.

Sam doesn't question it; he wastes no time in sitting on the edge of the hammock. He lays back in the shade of the trees, Ualani guiding him.

The faint strains of music drift quietly in from between the trees. Still smiling, Ualani begins to dance.

Sam watches the gentle sway of her hips, the undulations of her arms. The warm breeze caresses his face, and he is thinking that he has never felt so content, never so happy or fulfilled. He closes his eyes and drifts back into sleep.

* * *

Sam entered the shop with high spirits the next morning. Lamb was standing just outside the front office, and approached Sam as soon as he saw him.

"We have some things to go over. Get a cup of coffee or whatever you need to do, and meet me in my office in ten minutes."

Sam obeyed, taking care of his coat and pouring coffee into a Styrofoam cup. As he approached the closed

THE SHADY SIDE

door of Lamb's office, he could see through the windowed walls that Lamb was meeting with Carl Jessup, the Head Tech. Sam could only see Carl from the back as he approached, but he noticed that Carl was leaning forward in his chair, his portly body tense. Lamb's face was unsmiling, his dark eyebrows furrowed. His faced looked earnest as he spoke, shaking his head. He could hear the muffled sound of raised voices.

He was sipping his coffee when Carl suddenly stood and yanked the door open. He glared at Sam and shoved past him, pushing him against the wall. Sam just barely saved his coffee from spilling. He looked at Lamb, who waved him in.

"Sorry about that, Sam," said the older man.

"It's okay," Sam said.

"So we need to go over some procedures."

They spent the next hour going over the duties of Sam's new position. The rest of the day went quickly. His mood still buoyed by his sudden good fortune, Sam went out to warm up The Beast before leaving for the day.

Darkness had already fallen. The smell of cigarette smoke hung in the air, and Sam saw the bright red glowing tip of a cigarette in the darkness before he heard Carl Jessup's voice coming out of the shadows.

"Think you're hot stuff now, dontcha?" The voice slurred. "Only been at t'shop a month and a half, not even two months, and yer already the big shot."

Sam smelled the cloud of cigarette smoke combined with the pungent smell of alcohol on Carl's breath. "Look, Carl," Sam said, "I didn't ask for it. I never had an eye on your job."

"Save it," Carl slurred. "You had big ideas as soon as Lamb hired you."

"No, Carl. That isn't true."

"What, ya think I'm stupid? Of course it is. Ya had it in for me from day one. But don't expect it to last, kid." For the second time that day, Carl pushed past Sam. This time, Carl lost his balance and fell into Sam, crushing him against The Beast's driver side door.

Sam pushed against Carl, trying to heft the bigger man off of him.

Tim Shepherd came out of the shop. "Whoa, there!" he exclaimed. "Come on, big boy." He helped pull him off of Sam. "I'll call him a cab," Tim said. "You okay?"

Sam shrugged. "Yeah, I'm fine. No big deal, it could be worse."

"Well... you have a good night, Sam. We'll see you tomorrow."

"'Okay. See you tomorrow."

Sam slid behind the wheel of the Silverado, noting Ualani's always bright smile. He turned the key in the ignition.

Nothing. Not even a "click".

He tried again with no result. "What the hell?"

The worry line between his eyebrows deepened. He caught Ualani's eye. Her smile seemed somehow smaller, her expression darker. "Don't worry, Tiny Dancer. It's probably something simple."

He exited The Beast. Lifting the hood, he immediately saw the problem. The negative battery cable was unhooked. "That's weird," he mumbled to himself. "But more like not even right." He had changed his oil three days ago, checked his belts and hoses. The battery cables had been secure. But now the end of the negative cable lay atop the battery. The accompanying bolt lay neatly beside it.

At least it was an easy enough fix.

Before dropping the hood, Sam looked the engine over suspiciously, making sure that nothing else was out of place.

THE SHADY SIDE

He hopped back into The Beast, put the key in the ignition, turned it, and the engine roared to life. "See?" he addressed Ualani. "Nothing to it. Only thing hard about it is figuring out who the hell disconnected the cable. Because it's obvious that *someone* did. It didn't come off all on its own and then sit there on top of the battery, all laid out with the bolt."

He cranked up the heat, shivering. He had come out without his new winter coat, thinking he would only be outside for a few seconds, and the bitter cold was cutting through his dark blue button-down uniform shirt and the t-shirt he wore beneath it.

Ualani smiled her perpetual smile, which seemed to have returned to its normal brightness.

"Okay, I'm going in to grab my jacket and clean up. Back in a few minutes."

After he exited The Beast a second time and headed back into the shop, it occurred to Sam that he probably sounded like a crazy man. Talking to a *doll*.

The thought didn't stop Sam from talking to her again on his way home.

"Man, this is some thick shit," he commented. Big, soft snowflakes hurtled out of the darkness toward his windshield, where they promptly melted and the wipers wiped them away over and over again. The sheer volume of bright white snowflakes created a wall that blocked his vision and threatened to blind him, and Sam found himself slowing The Beast down to a crawl, hunching over slightly to peer through the windshield.

"What if it was Jessup?" he asked Ualani. "He was standing in the shadows right next to The Beast when I came out to warm her up. And he was pissed at me because Lamb got rid of him and gave me his job. It seems logical that Jessup would want to fuck with me."

As he passed a car that had gone off the road into the ditch, Sam noticed a pair of bright headlights coming up fast behind him. He gently eased his vehicle out of the way, stopping temporarily on the shoulder to let the vehicle pass. He then pulled back onto the road.

"Nope," he said to Ualani, "I'm in no hurry. Someone else wants to race down this thing, more power to 'em. It won't be *me* in the ditch. We're going to stay laid back and take our time."

Ualani bobbed happily in agreement. Her smile seemed to have grown, stretching almost from ear to ear.

"Glad you approve of that plan, Ma'am," Sam told her, touching his cap briefly.

About one hundred feet later, Sam passed the car he had pulled over for. It had slid into the ditch.

"See, Tiny Dancer?" Sam beamed proudly. He couldn't place the source of his happiness. He was crawling along through a snowstorm, The Beast had been tampered with, and the man whose job he had taken was pissed at him and most likely had a plan to go with his sense of having been betrayed.

Maybe it was because yesterday, Sam had been sleeping in a freezing cold apartment. His old, worn boots had been taped together with duct tape, he'd had no food or money, and wasn't expecting his situation to change for a very long time - and today, Sam had a brand-new pair of cozy winter boots, a warm new jacket, a great job with good pay, and a real apartment where he could turn up the heat if it got cold; not to mention a refrigerator full of food.

All this since he had set Ualani on his dashboard. Was he just being superstitious? He didn't know. But he damned well planned to toe the line, especially if doing the things he was supposed to do continued to earn him rewards.

He made it home safely, taking an extra twenty minutes to do so. The only part of Ualani that moved was her upper body, just as it was supposed to. She didn't slide around as Sam had expected her to, but stayed firmly planted where he had positioned her on the dashboard.

He curled up that night between his warm flannel sheets and full belly and promptly fell asleep.

* * *

The dream always starts the same.

The warm breeze blows white, sandy ripples across the beach. The sun beats down, burning his pale shoulders and the backs of his legs.

Kaho Ali is walking out in the ocean, far past the mangroves. There are no whales around him, today. His strides create rolling waves. He turns and gives Sam a huge, toothy grin and a thumbs-up sign.

Sam turns and sees Ualani approaching. She is wearing her customary friendly smile. There is no sign of the darkness he had seen on Ualani's carved wooden face the evening before. He watches the sway of her hips appreciatively as she nears him.

He expects her to take his hand and lead him in a stroll down the beach, or maybe to the hammock in the trees. Instead, she puts her arms around his neck and kisses him fully on the lips.

For a second, he is so surprised that he forgets to react. This is the first time that Ualani has indicated she had more interest in Sam other than simply being his friendly, beautiful, graceful... cheerleader. Because that is what she has seemed like. Support. Encouragement.

Not romance.

Now, the feel of her arms around him, her body pressed against his, the lush scent of her fresh orchid wreath and leis drift sweetly up his nose. He is lost in her kiss, her lips full and soft. His heart is racing, his palms are sweaty, and he has grown painfully hard, pushing against her.

But below the surface of his desire, he feels, maybe for the first time since he was a small child – safe. Content. Happy.
Loved?
Yes. Maybe... loved.
And he knows he never wants this dream to end. He doesn't want to go back into the cold of the unforgiving upstate New York winter. He wants to stay here, on this beach – wherever it is. He wants to see how far he will be able to go with Ualani.
But now, she breaks the kiss and lays her cheek against Sam's. Her lips are close to his ear, and for the first time, he hears Ualani's voice, a soft whisper:
"Watch out."

* * *

Sam woke in his warm bed between his soft flannel sheets. He stretched, reluctant to get up and start the day, but he urgently needed to use the bathroom.

He felt something scratchy against his feet. He sat up, pulled the blankets aside, and looked.

Just as he had found the day that he moved out of his old place, sprinkled on and around his feet between the sheets at the foot of his bed were fine grains of white sand.

Dream-Ualani's kiss had felt so real: the pressure of her full, soft lips against his; the firm fragility of her small frame pressed into his. He felt it again and again as he relived the scene in his memory; and a shadowy, dark, but not unpleasant sensation washed slowly through him and settled in as the day progressed. He tried to keep his focus on his work to stave off his physical discomfort.

About six inches of snow had fallen the night before. The morning sun sparkled on the untouched surface as Sam went to warm up The Beast. As he walked, he kicked up the pristine powder in small white clouds.

THE SHADY SIDE

The Beast started right up.

"Damn," he told Ualani, smiling from his dashboard. "It's so cold. You must be freezing wearing that," he said, indicating her pink bikini top, grass skirt, and bare feet and legs.

He smiled a rueful smile. He was talking to the hula dancer as though she was a living person. His dreams had begun to stick with him. She appeared in them, for whatever reason. Maybe it was all the changes he'd being experiencing.

She's just a wooden doll, he thought to himself.

And that was exactly part of the problem.

Maybe he needed a girlfriend; he had gone too long without female company, and could be that was translating into his dreams.

He shook his head. He had to remember, that's all they were: dreams.

But there was the matter of the sand on his sheets. Where had it come from?

As soon as he pulled out of his driveway and drove down the snow-packed street, he felt the Silverado pulling to the right and heard the telltale *bump-bump-bump*.

He pulled over and exited The Beast. Sure enough, he had a flat tire.

Squatting beside his truck, he scanned the tire, but found no nails or other indicators of a puncture. He checked the valve stem and saw that the cover was missing. Upon closer inspection, he saw that the stem was bent so extremely that it had put pressure on the valve, releasing the air.

"Damn it!" Sam stood.

On the one hand, he was glad that the tire itself didn't appear damaged. Smith Mountain Gas was not three blocks away, and he could nurse The Beast to the gas station and fill up the tire. Easy-peasy.

Irritation had begun to gnaw at him, however. Valve stem covers were a dime a dozen; losing one was as easy as losing one sock from a pair. But how had the stem gotten so badly bent?

Sam shook his head. He didn't have time for this now. He needed to get to work. He got back into The Beast and drove slowly to the air pump. He grabbed a set of pliers out of the box and bent the stem back into place. He filled the tire, then rummaged in his tool box for some electrical tape. He tore off a piece and wrapped the stem, covering the opening. He would grab a new cover at work. He might have to replace the valve stem, as well.

He hopped back into The Beast. He glanced at Ualani as he turned the key. Her face somehow looked a little different. Concerned?

"It's just a thing, Ualani," he said. "Let's keep our fingers crossed. It should be okay. I hope."

Talking to a doll again, he thought. *I'd better not let the guys at work catch me doing that.*

He was preoccupied on his drive to work, barely registering Ualani on his dashboard in her pink bikini top, reaching for him with her outstretched hand. If he had noticed her, he would have seen the frown darkening her pretty features.

He failed to see the school bus ahead of him or the line of cars stopped behind it until it was almost too late. He hit the brakes. The truck bed slid sideways as it stopped barely two feet short of the car in front of him. Ualani slid several inches forward on the dashboard, tipping up on the front edge of her little black stand and falling over on her face.

Panicked, Sam reached for the hula doll and set her upright. "Ualani! I'm sorry, I'm so sorry, I wasn't paying attention, I was distracted! I didn't mean for you to get hurt!" He felt a sudden, sharp pain in his finger. "Ouch! What the fuck?"

THE SHADY SIDE

He looked at his index finger and saw a bead of blood forming. He looked at the hula dancer. She stared back at him, accusation in her eyes, the friendly smile gone, a blood-smeared frown in its place.

Ualani had bitten him!

"I'm sorry," Sam said nervously. He looked away as he reached for the packet of tissues in his center console.

When he glanced back at Ualani, her smile had returned, the blood had disappeared from her lips.

He blinked and stared at the small face. It was just like the time Sam thought Ualani had winked at him. He had thought that maybe he had imagined it.

Had he imagined it this time, as well?

He looked at his finger. The blood still welled from the tiny wound.

The line of cars ahead of Sam started moving once again and Sam's focus returned to the road. He and his small passenger arrived at Lamb's Auto without further incident.

Since Lamb had fired Carl Jessup, he was directly supervising Sam's training as Head Tech. The demands of his training and the busy work day pushed concerns of that morning's incident to the back of Sam's mind. Every now and again, however, Sam looked at the small self-adhesive bandage on his finger and remembered how it was injured.

He felt less disturbed about the manner of injury as the day flew by, however. Maybe Ualani hadn't bitten him. Maybe there was something in her grass skirt that had jabbed him, or there was an unseen splinter poking out of her wooden construction somewhere that had caused the cut.

By the time Lamb's closed, Sam had convinced himself that it was just a freak accident.

He went out to The Beast just after darkness had fallen to warm her up. He turned the key and gave it a little gas.

"Vroooooomm!" The sound of the muffler roaring nearly startled him out of his skin.

He exited the cab. He could smell exhaust fumes. On his hands and knees, he held his breath and peered underneath the truck at the exhaust system.

Somehow, the studs that connected the flanges between the catalytic converter and intermediate pipe had come loose. He could see where they lay on the ground. The two separated ends hung down opposite one another. "Son of a *bitch!*"

"What's going on, Sam?"

Sam stood up to see Tim Shepherd looking at him inquiringly beneath the yellow glow of one of the parking lot lights. His hands were tucked into the pockets of his black parka; his pale face hovered inside the hood of a black sweatshirt he wore beneath the winter coat, pulled up over his thick, blonde hair.

"Exhaust came apart a little bit," Sam said.

"I thought she sounded a little louder than usual when you started her up."

Sam scratched his head. "I don't understand it," he said. "Seems to be one thing, right after another, the past couple of days."

"You want to bring her in and put her on the lift?'

"Is that okay?"

"Well yes, it's after hours. We're closed."

"All right, then. It looks like everything is there that needs to be. Just the studs came out of the flanges."

"Sounds simple enough. Take us five minutes. Bring her in." Tim beckoned with his arm and headed back into the shop to open the bay door for Sam.

The fix took closer to ten minutes. The two men stood talking afterward.

THE SHADY SIDE

"You think someone is sabotaging you?" Tim asked after Sam gave him a brief recap of the past couple of days.

Sam shrugged. "I don't know what's going on. Either it's just a string of freak coincidences, or someone has a bug up their ass."

Tim looked at him with cool, sea-green eyes. "Who do you think it could be?"

Sam waved his hand dismissively. "I don't want to go around accusing anyone. I really don't know. Jessup was a little aggressive with me the other night, but I can't say that it was him."

"Ever thought of investing in an alarm?"

"On *The Beast*? The alarm itself would have more value."

Tim laughed and slapped Sam on the back. "Take 'er easy. See you tomorrow."

"Yeah. Thanks for the help."

Tim saluted him.

Ualani looked at him, her friendly smile inscrutable, as Sam slid behind the wheel. He drove out and Tim lowered the bay door behind him. As he pulled away, the interior shop lights darkened.

* * *

Dark clouds roll into the sky over the peaceful island setting, blotting out the bright sun that Sam has grown accustomed to. The pale blue waters have taken on a darker, stormier shade. A strong wind blows the tops of the mangroves and hala trees.

Kaho Ali—Counselor Kaho Ali, not giant dream Koho Ali—sits at a polished wooden table graced with a dinner setting for one. He rests with his legs stretched out casually before him, one ankle crossed over the other, leaning back, fingers laced behind his head. A fine white linen napkin folded into a shape of a swan sits perched at the center of the plate.

Kaho sees Sam and gives him an unsmiling nod. Sam's stomach sinks at the big man's somber expression.

Sam turns. Ualani stands behind him, her head bowed. He steps toward her and reaches out his hand, touching her arm. She slowly lifts her head and looks at him with an expression of profound sadness, her dark brown almond eyes drooping at the corners, her full, soft lips thinned into a hard line. Sam knows she is upset because of the accident that morning.

"Ualani, I'm sorry. I wasn't angry, I was distracted. It was an accident."

He touches her hand, and as he looks upon her face, her brown eyes lighten, changing to gold. Her round, black pupils narrow into vertical slits. Her lips widen, stretching wider and wider into a grotesque, elongated smile. Her pearl-white teeth narrow into lethal half-inch spikes that protrude crookedly from her mouth.

Goosebumps rise on Sam's flesh despite the unforgiving heat of the oceanic sun. He takes an involuntary step backward. "No Ualani, please, it was an accident, I wasn't trying to hurt anyone, I swear-"

The smells of old fish and rot emanate from Ualani's mouth, covering up the lush floral aroma of her leis. She closes her small hand around his, digging her sharp nails into his skin, crushing his finger bones with an iron grip. He tries to pull away, but she holds on, pulling Sam closer to her. Her lips curl outward in a snarl as she rears her head, prepared to plunge her teeth into his throat—

* * *

A faint noise woke Sam. He threw back the covers and left his bed, feeling the wet sand his feet left behind on his bottom sheet. He ran to the living room window, which faced the parking lot.

The moon was nearly full, and beneath its sun-reflected glow, Sam saw someone kneeling beside The Beast. The figure in the dark jacket, hood pulled up over his head, seemed somehow familiar to him.

Sam had his hands on the window frame, ready to push the window open and yell at the kneeling figure, but he caught himself. If he yelled out the window, it would give the guy a chance to get away.

He stuffed his feet into his boots and threw his coat on. He slammed his door behind him and ran down the hall to the stairwell; he took the steps two at a time.

The quiet, frigid night amplified the sounds of Sam's footfalls pounding down the stairs, even outside the building. The kneeling man heard him before he reached the bottom landing, and when Sam opened the front door, all he saw was the back of the fleeing saboteur, who had already made it to the end of the small parking lot and was now halfway down the driveway entrance.

"Hey!" Sam's shout echoed through the parking lot, even though he knew that calling out was futile.

He went to stand beside The Beast and smelled the distinct odor of gasoline. He walked to the opposite side of The Beast and saw the hose and gas can.

"God*dammit!*" Sam kicked the gas can. "Fuck this!" He pulled his keys from his jacket pocket, unlocked The Beast, and jumped in. He started her up, revved the gas, and switched on both the defroster and the windshield wipers. The windshield hadn't frozen over yet; only a thin layer of frost covered the glass. The air coming from the vent, cold as it was, started clearing circles on the windshield as he gunned it through the parking lot to the road. He slowed, his eyes scanning to the right and left down the brightly lit, deserted street. He had lost precious time; the saboteur had disappeared from sight.

"Damn it!" He pounded his steering wheel with his fist.

Ualani looked at him reproachfully from her place on the dashboard. Her smile had disappeared.

He looked back at her defiantly; yet the memory of his recent nightmare made him keep his voice calm and even. "Don't get your skirt in a bunch, Tiny Dancer," he said. "It's cool. I'm not out to hurt anyone. I just want to catch this guy."

Sam blanched when Ualani's expression darkened further. He steeled himself. *It was only a dream,* he assured himself. *She's still just a wooden doll. It's not like she can really hurt you.*

He was about to nose The Beast out into the street, but something made him pause. He sat, his foot on the brake, letting the Silverado idle quietly. It had only been a few seconds between the moment Sam had seen the guy and the moment he had reached the end of the driveway. The guy couldn't have gotten that far. He had to be close by.

The streetlights reflected off of the snow, making the white expanse bright as day. Sam switched his headlights off and found that he could see just fine without them on. If the saboteur was nearby, Sam didn't want his headlights to give him away.

After a few minutes of waiting, Sam began to get impatient. *Fuck, I may as well start cruising and look for this guy.*

At that moment, his wait was rewarded with the sound of a motor firing into life. He stayed his position for a few more seconds, and soon he saw the twin beams of a pair of headlights pulling out of the Smith Mountain Gas parking lot down the street. He put the Silverado in reverse and backed her up a few feet, into the shadows of the trees that bordered the driveway entrance.

THE SHADY SIDE

Sam watched intently, waiting for the vehicle to pass so that he could determine whether its driver was the guy who had been siphoning gas from The Beast.

The car, a black Chevy Malibu, cruised slowly by. The driver turned his head and looked down the driveway and into the parking lot of Sam's apartment house.

A pale face peering out of a dark hoodie, covered by a thicker black parka.

In the bright streetlights, Sam was able to make out the features of a face he recognized.

It was Tim Shepherd.

"What the *fuck?*" Sam breathed as he watched from the shadows.

Feeling a sudden burst of rage, he floored the gas pedal. Snow plumed out behind The Beast's tires as they attempted to gain traction in the snow, below which the pavement was covered in glare ice. The Beast lurched forward from her hiding place in the shadows. As she picked up speed, careening out into the road, Sam saw Tim's eyes go wide and his mouth open in an "O". Tim sped up, trying to get out of Sam's way, but it was too late.

The Beast's front bumper clipped the rear right fender of the Malibu, turning the smaller vehicle sideways so that it came to rest positioned across the street's center line. The impact turned the Silverado at an angle and he overshot the other vehicle, heading for the thick wall of snow that the plows had built on the side of the road. Sam slammed the brake and cranked the wheel to the left, pulling The Beast into a power slide to avoid the snow bank. She halted behind the Malibu, in the left lane, facing the wrong direction.

The spin sent Ualani flying off of the dashboard. Her body separated at the waist into two pieces as she landed on the passenger side of The Beast's bench seat. The hula dancer's pretty features twisted into an ugly snarl.

But Sam wasn't paying attention.

The Malibu's driver maneuvered the car gently out of its position with a light application of his foot to the gas pedal, giving it the minimum amount of pressure needed to guide the car forward without skidding and sliding. He swung the car back in the direction from which he had come, toward Smith Mountain Gas, in the opposite direction that Sam's Silverado was facing.

Sam cursed. Angry and no longer thinking clearly, he cranked the wheel and stomped his gas pedal, attempting to swing The Beast around in a U-turn and follow the Malibu. He gave The Beast too much gas, and her tires spun on the ice below the packed snow.

Breathing deeply, Sam put the truck in reverse, swung the wheel, and tapped the gas pedal lightly. The truck bed swung around to the left. He turned the wheels to the right, again applied light pressure to the gas pedal, and The Beast gained traction and moved easily in Sam's second attempt at a U-turn.

The Malibu's rear lights glowed red ahead of him. Sam dared to lean more heavily on the gas pedal, gritting his teeth and thanking God for zero traffic at this early morning hour. He failed to notice the two pieces of the wooden hula dancer's body inching toward one another on the seat beside him.

The Malibu wasn't that far ahead of Sam; he felt The Beast's tires grip the pavement as she rolled onto a long section that had been cleared of snow and ice. He stepped on the gas pedal, racing to gain ground between himself and Tim.

Tim Shepherd. *Why?*

He was sure as hell going to find out.

There wasn't enough distance to gain a lot of speed before The Beast's nose slammed into the Malibu's rear end.

THE SHADY SIDE

Again, the force pushed the Malibu to the right, jackknifing from The Beast's front bumper. Sam cranked the wheel to the right, relentlessly keeping on the Malibu's tail, finally shoving the front of the smaller Chevy into a snow bank, pushing its hood up and folding it in half. Steam hissed from the Malibu's exposed engine.

Sam threw the Silverado into park, fumbled his seat belt off, and exited the cab. He slipped and slid on the snow at the street's shoulder.

Ualani pushed herself up from The Beast's seat into a standing position.

Inside the Malibu, a dazed and shaken Tim Shepherd attempted to hit the lock button, but he wasn't fast enough. Sam yanked his door open, leaned over him to release his seatbelt, and dragged Tim from the driver seat. Sam threw him against the Malibu and grabbed the hood of his sweatshirt, using it to slam Tim's head against the top of his car.

Rather than put Tim down, the blow enraged him. He turned his body, elbowing Sam viciously in the solar plexus. Sam gasped for breath and lost his footing. He fell backward onto his ass, sustaining a flare of white-hot pain as his tail bone hit the ground and bent. The frozen wetness of the snow-packed road seeped through his pajama bottoms.

"You little asshole!" Tim launched himself at Sam, bent over him and grabbed the front of Sam's coat. He slammed the back of Sam's head against the road. "How do *you* like it?"

"What the fuck is wrong with you?" Sam screamed. *"I didn't do a fucking thing to you!"*

He grabbed Tim's forearms, spreading them outward like wings. Tim fell forward on top of Sam, who rolled sideways, dumping Tim off his chest and onto the street.

"How could you not know, you piece of *garbage?* Are you really that self-involved?" Tim scrambled to try to get to his knees before Sam knocked him down. The two grappled, covered in greasy, salty, winter road-mud. "That Head Tech job was *mine!* I busted my *ass* for six years to get that position. And you walked in and had it! Like *that!*" Adding extra emphasis, Tim knocked Sam back to the ground.

"Really, you shithead? *That's* what all this bullshit is about? Jesus, man, why didn't you just fucking *say* something, instead of sabotaging my truck?" Before Tim could get at him again, Sam bent his knee, placed his boot squarely in Tim's chest, and was ready to shove him away, when he saw that Tim's pale face had gone even whiter. He looked over Sam's head with wide, terrified eyes.

"W-w-what is *that?*" Tim whispered.

Looking at the man's face, all of Sam's hairs stood on end.

He smelled the lush scent of fresh orchids, out of place in the deep winter snowscape.

With a feeling of dread, afraid of what he was going to see, he lowered his foot, propped himself up on his elbows, and looked behind him.

"Ualani," he whispered.

A life-sized Ualani, the hula dancer of Sam's dreams, was climbing down from The Beast's cab. Dressed in only her bikini top and grass skirt, she should have been freezing; but there was a red nimbus of light around her, and wherever her bare feet stepped, the snow melted, hissing steam into the frigid air.

Her face was twisted with rage. Her brown irises turned gold; her round pupils elongated vertically. Her lips widened into those of a bloodthirsty nightmare clown; her spiked teeth stuck out haphazardly, but lethally, from between them.

THE SHADY SIDE

She strode toward the two men. The smell of rotted fish and death wafted toward them, accompanied by the sickeningly sweet smell of her leis and orchid crown.

Tim Shepard fell back, kneeling. He crossed himself. "Our Father, who art in Heaven, hallowed be thy name..." he began, whispering.

Sam began crab-walking backwards. "Please, *please*, Ualani, *Tiny Dancer,* please, no, I didn't mean it," he whimpered. His pleas fell on deaf ears.

"You never mean it!" Ualani's voice was deep and distorted, not a woman's voice, but a reverberating demon's shout. She looked to the night sky above and screamed a deep, unearthly scream.

She bent over, and with one hand, grabbed Sam by the front of his jacket, plucked him off the pavement, and held him over her head.

Seeing Ualani's monster visage so close paralyzed him. His eyes widened with terror, ready to pop from their sockets, and his jaw worked soundlessly, a string of saliva hanging from the corner of his mouth.

Ualani screamed again. The clear night sky instantly filled with clouds. Thunder boomed directly overhead and lightning forked across the sky, which opened to release a deluge of rain.

She lowered Sam and tore his throat out with her teeth. Blood spurted from his jugular and drenched Ualani's face. The sudden downpour washed the blood down her body.

She tossed him to the ground and fell upon him, her spiked teeth puncturing through his jacket, the inhuman strength of her jaw pushing them through, tearing through flesh and cartilage, cracking through rib bones.

Tim Shepherd, no longer reciting the Lord's Prayer, slowly rose to his feet. He moved as silently as he could, hoping to slip away without drawing the monster's attention.

She caught his movement from the corner of her eye and suddenly swiveled her head to look at him, her face covered in gore and purple and red chunks; pieces of Sam's heart and lungs.

She snarled at Tim and rose.

He backed away, arms outstretched, palms facing outward as though he could ward her off.

"Please," he begged, backing away. "I don't know you, I didn't do anything to you, I swear,"

Suddenly, she was there, directly in front of him, a gore-spattered nightmare clad in a delicate pink bikini top, an authentic grass skirt, and a crown and leis of fresh orchids.

Ualani stepped forward to claim him.

The heavens wept.

* * *

The city of Smith Mountain Park flooded that morning. The torrential downpour that occurred during the one o'clock hour melted the six-foot high snow banks piled alongside the roads, as well as the three-foot deep covering that had blanketed most of the area.

The bodies of two men were found washed down West Main Street, over one hundred yards from where their vehicles had apparently collided right around the time that the deluge had begun. The two deceased then had to be identified by their respective vehicles and their teeth, as there was barely enough left of their bodies to be identified. These had been torn apart, and their hearts, as well as several other muscles and organs, had been summarily ripped from the bodies by what looked like the teeth of some vicious animal.

Strangest of all, the two men's eyes had both been removed – but with care.

* * *

THE SHADY SIDE

A human-size Kahoali sat at his pristine beachside table, admiring the elegant table setting. He leaned forward, smelling the white blossoms of the flower that had been placed in a vase as the centerpiece.

"Ah, this is the life, is it not, my beautiful Ualani?"

The dancer smiled as her arms and fingers moved in delicate gestures, her hips swaying gracefully in time to the music.

Her dance told the story of Kahoali, her revered Ocean God.

"Here we are!" Kahoali's face beamed happily as his serving boy set the bowl of kava on his plate; then the boy bowed and backed away. Kahoali picked up his spoon and slurped gently. "Perfect! You have done well, my love. I trust you enjoyed your own repast?"

Ualani smiled again and nodded, never missing a movement in her dance.

He consulted the open laptop next to his plate. "Where shall we go next, hmm, Ualani? Not so far inland, I don't think. What about Massachusetts? I have heard many things about Boston drivers. Boston is coastal. Yes, I think Massachusetts will do just fine."

He dipped his spoon into his kava, capturing an object onto the curved surface. Lifting the spoon to his lips, he slurped the eyeball with the watery-blue colored iris into his mouth. He closed his teeth on it, and it popped like a cherry tomato. He chewed it and made contented noises.

He rolled his eyes. "What a delightful delicacy. Worth waiting for. And *four* of them, this time. Ualani, you are *so* good to me." He slurped another eyeball, this one with a sea-green iris, from his spoon.

"All the doodah day," he hummed.

A BRAND-NEW GIRL

APRIL

Jessie James Mason checked her pedometer. She had walked just over three miles; not enough. She would have to walk the trails she hadn't travelled yet in order to meet her quota, and to burn enough calories to contribute to the melting of the extra inches from her oversized breasts, bulging belly, and the cellulite on her thighs.

She had switched from drinking soda to water, had cut sugary snacks and candy from her diet, and had reduced her food consumption by a third at every meal. She had been doing the speed walking every day for a month and a half, and had only lost three pounds.

It wasn't enough weight lost, fast enough. JJ was tired of wearing baggy shirts to hide the bulges; tired of having to size by trial and error when buying bras online because no brick-and-mortar retail stores carried her size.

She had known when she began this that it would take time and patience. She knew she would have to work hard to lose the extra inches. She knew the exercise and eating healthier were good for her body and for her mind.

Progress just seemed to take so long that it sometimes frustrated her.

She came to the next fork and chose the path that bore to the right. It would take her deeper into the woods, around the back of Kingfisher Park, to the swampy area and the long boardwalk that tilted downward along its right edge.

JJ had long since built up a sweat slick that coated her entire body. The morning temperature was warm for early spring. She had made the right decision to go out at sunrise, while it was still cool. Even so, she was happy for the warmer weather. The mud along the trails had finally dried up, and it was no longer necessary to pick her way around the sludgy puddles.

The new buds on the trees had begun to open, providing a little shade against the bright sunlight, while casting a ripe green tint to the interior of Kingfisher Park. She hadn't brought her camera today. The last couple of times she had come, it was more to observe the spring wildlife on the move along the paths she'd put aside during the bitter winter, in favor of her indoor workout mat, stationary bike, and hand weights.

She'd gotten some excellent photos of a family of ducklings, a beaver, turtles sunning themselves on a log in the pond, deer, and numerous chipmunks.

But the camera was heavy and the strap was too short, making the device difficult to walk with because it didn't hang comfortably. Today she had left it home so that she could get some productive mileage in, rather than the stop-and-go wandering she fell into when taking photos.

She checked her cell phone. Not even 7:30, yet. She would have plenty of time to finish up her walk and get back home to have breakfast and a shower before she had to be to work.

Work. JJ preferred not to think about her current employment. She worked part-time as a cashier at the local SuperFry, but the work was unfulfilling and the pay was less than she would like. It just wasn't a good match.

She pushed the negative thoughts away and focused on her breathing. Soon she would have a different job. She'd been sending out at least three resumes per day during the past few weeks, and had already interviewed with several companies. The financial slump she was in would be over, and she would be able to pay her bills and maybe be able to *live* instead of just survive, hanging on by a frayed and unraveling thread.

She reached the tilted boardwalk and sped up, stepping as fast as she could. She was on the last part of the walk. After the boardwalk there would be a curve left, then right, and she would emerge from the dense woods onto the trailhead that opened onto the parking lot; but right now, she pushed as hard as she could. Her heart felt like a triphammer drumming inside her rib cage.

Something big flew out from between the surrounding trees and hit JJ in the face. She thought it was a bird, at first – a duck from the swamp, maybe, that had flown into her by accident.

It had wings, a fuzzy body that covered her torso and right shoulder, where it landed. When she saw the black, shiny softball-sized eyes looking into her own, the antennae sticking up from its head, swiveling around curiously, she screamed and tried to slap the thing away. It clung to her T-shirt and to the skin of her right arm with barbs that protruded from where its feet should have been. It had what seemed like a million legs wrapped around her, but there were only six, covered with sharp, spiky hairs. The barbs and the hairs stuck into her skin like needles.

THE SHADY SIDE

JJ screamed, pushing at the velvety body, trying to dislodge the thing, but it refused to let go. Beneath the velvet-covered torso, the thing was hard as a rock. Four transparent wings, similar to those of a dragonfly, beat her about the face and shoulders, moving so fast that they were nearly a blur. They dislodged her earbuds. She could hear the high-pitched whining sound their motion made.

The creature's stinger plunged into JJ's lower abdomen. The white-hot searing pain rendered her mute, though her mouth was open wide in a scream. She dropped like a rock to the boardwalk.

The giant insect, having completed its business, left its stinger lodged in JJ's abdomen and flew clumsily back into Kingfisher Park swamp. It was dead by nightfall.

JUNE

Spine straight. Shoulders back, elbows in, butt tucked in. Core engaged; roll the hips, roll the foot, heel-to-toe, heel-to-toe. And the whole time, she was supposed to keep her body relaxed.

Breathe.

Damn, JJ thought. *There's so much to remember to do to walk right, I can't enjoy it!*

She never used to have to think about it. Up until two months ago, walking had been as natural as breathing.

Now, her body felt awkward and uncomfortably alien. Her shoulders were tense, reminding her to relax them. Again. It was like a game. Remember to move and position her body correctly as she walked; forget and tense up, start slouching, forget to breathe the right way; then self-correct and start from the beginning.

JJ had been walking this stretch of Hadley Road every day for the past two months. She had grown bored of it.

This three-mile stretch of rural road was predominantly straight and flat, interrupted only by a couple of slight knolls. It cut through an expanse of empty fields edged by woods in the distance. Other than that, there were only a few houses dotted here and there across the landscape. Nothing much of interest to look at.

The sun was still low, having broken the horizon only an hour before; it was still chilly enough to raise goosebumps across her flesh. She knew that the temperature would soar by mid-morning, and she would end the return walk with a layer of sweat clinging to her skin.

The cloudless deep blue sky stretched infinitely above. The morning belonged only to JJ; to her and the birds twittering their happy morning songs.

She heard a vehicle approaching from behind her, in the distance. She raised her phone and pushed the camera button and reversed the view so that she could use the device as a rear-view mirror.

Still quite far back, the approaching vehicle looked too big to be a car. It was white.

JJ walked on at a steady pace and checked her phone camera every now and again.

Yes, it was definitely a van. It looked like the same van that had passed her walking every day for the past several weeks. Sometimes it passed her twice, traveling in either direction. It had no rear or side windows.

She felt, more than thought, a question flit through her mind. An energy source in itself, it grew and spread downward through her throat, her chest, her stomach, legs, and filled her feet.

THE SHADY SIDE

The question echoed through her mind: *Will today be the day?* She tried to push down the desperate hope that tried to rise into her heart.

She was hungry. The hunger was a great yawning emptiness inside of her. She had been ignoring it for a long time, now.

JJ had often thought about just doing it, finding someone at night, alone on the street. But she didn't want to feed in the street, and not just any food would satisfy her cravings. To eat what was destined to be her new menu, she needed privacy. She needed security.

She knew what would happen if she were discovered. If she wasn't killed outright, she would be experimented on until her body gave out.

JJ wasn't ready to die just because of a freak accident. It wasn't *her* fault she'd been attacked by some mutated giant insect.

She made a show of adjusting her earbuds and her mp3 player. The mp3 player wasn't turned on.

She breathed deeply, rhythmically, corrected her body, and walked on.

The vehicle approached... and slowed. JJ risked a glimpse into her phone screen, checking the expanse of road that stretched behind her. It was empty of any other approaching traffic. No bicycles or pedestrians. The section of road that continued ahead of her was equally desolate. She could see where Hadley Road ended in a "T" where it met West Hadley Road about a quarter mile ahead. The stop sign was still too far away to see.

It was only JJ and the windowless white van on the three-mile stretch of road.

She kept walking, pretending to be oblivious, listening to music, fiddling with her phone, while trying to stay calm and focused.

She felt his thoughts come through to her, then. They felt like a tender bruise, edged in blood, dark with intent.

The intent came through loud and clear to JJ. He may as well have shouted his plans. He was excited.

He was Crannich Yusev. He intended to take her, torture her, and kill her.

She heard the crunch of gravel as the van rolled up behind her and stopped.

I guess today will *be the day.*

The vehicle remained idling. JJ listened to the driver side door open. It didn't close. Then came the sound of the side cargo door sliding open. Footsteps, approaching her from behind. She glanced one last time into her phone, the brief glimpse registering the man's image in her mind.

Not a tall man. About 5'8". In his late 50s. Dark-blonde hair gone gray, buzz-cut. Once-muscular upper body grown lean with age, except for the stomach, which had gone to pot, creating a pregnant-looking bulge beneath generic gray custodial uniform-type coveralls. Round cop-like sunglasses, behind which JJ knew were ice-blue eyes.

He's not very obvious, at all, she thought sarcastically.

He held a pistol in his hand, pointed at her. The safety was still on.

She timed her move perfectly. Her would-be-assailant's arms closed on empty air as she ducked and stepped back to the left behind him, gripping his wrist and pulling it with her as she reversed. She yanked his arm up behind him in a chicken wing, easily disarming him. His pistol clattered on the pavement. In a heartbeat, JJ had the point of her switchblade against the man's jugular.

Yusev cried out as she squeezed the tender narrow spot between his neck and shoulder in a cruel grip, putting him on his knees. She poked the point of her blade into his neck, enough to draw blood but not enough to injure. He needed to know she meant business, but she couldn't afford to hurt him severely. Not yet. She had to keep him fresh.

"Pick it up," JJ said. "By the barrel. Hand it to me." She kept the blade firmly against his throat, bending with him as he reached for the gun. She didn't bother to threaten. She liked to let the knife speak for itself.

She took the gun from him, switched the safety off and cocked it, pushing the business end firmly against the side of his head.

"Get up. Hurry up, before someone comes. Who else is in the van?"

The man's voice was shaky. "N-no one."

JJ knew no one else was in the van.

"Don't fucking lie to me!" JJ felt a rush of adrenaline as she poked her blade into his bare bicep.

"*No one, no one, I swear!*"

"Get back in the van! Through the cargo door. Climb up into the driver seat. *Hurry up!*" JJ looked up and down the road. Still empty.

With her blade at his neck, holding his own gun to his head, JJ pushed against him, kneeing him in the back of the leg, steering him toward the van's gaping cargo door. As he was climbing in, he suddenly twisted and kicked at her. JJ cracked him on the ankle with his pistol. He cried out, and she viciously stuck her knife into the meat of his calf.

"Ah, *shit!*"

"Get in and cut the crap! Get in the driver's seat. *Drive!*"

"What the *fuck?*"

"Shut up! Put on your seatbelt! *Drive!*"

Keeping the gun trained on Yusev, JJ wiped her bloodied blade on the upholstery of the seat behind his head. She snapped it closed and folded her fingers down toward her wrist, deftly tucking the knife into her wristband.

She inhaled deeply, smelling the fresh scent of the blood. She forced herself to breathe deeply to calm her pounding heart.

She watched Yusev start the van as she reached behind her and slid the cargo door shut. It engaged with a satisfying slam.

"Take me where you were gonna take me. Drive normal. Don't attract any attention."

Yusev's killing room was located four hours away. JJ prepared herself mentally for the drive. She prayed that she could keep her hunger controlled for the duration of the trip – and that she wouldn't pass out from malnourishment before the time came.

She perched on the edge of the bench seat behind him, leaning forward against the back of the driver seat, where she could see his face in the rearview and where his hands were in view. The black scanner mounted above the rearview spewed static and chatter; the radar detector beside it remained quiet.

She knew without looking around her that the back of Yusef's van was clean and neat as a pin, except for the black bag. It contained zip ties, duct tape, a tarp, and various tools; standard serial killer fare.

She knew his house was the same way. Compulsively clean. Overly sterile. There was an underlying smell beneath the bleach. It was the smell of blood and terror.

But not his killing room. Not where he took his girls. That room was splattered with layers of old blood. The blood, the sweat, and the fear had stiffened the old stained mattress where he chained his victims down to the wall.

Yusev protested, "I wasn't going to do anything! I wasn't going to hurt you, I sw –"

THE SHADY SIDE

Thunk! Yusev's pistol connected with his skull. He cringed forward and the van jerked in it's lane. "Don't talk! Just *drive.*"

JJ could feel his thoughts, as well as every one of his tensed muscles, every twitch his body made.

He had a few little holes in him from her knife, but it was his ego that was wounded. He couldn't wrap his head around what had just happened. Though he kept his composure, his rage boiled just beneath the surface. He didn't yet have enough sense to fear her.

He was the predator. *She* was the prey. His sensitive pride was already scheming, had already vowed, that *he* would be the victor. He was experienced; he'd been doing this a long time. And this girl was – what? A vigi*lante*. An amateur. A *girl*. No, not even that. A *thing*. Living meat to play with until she wore out.

Yusef would never see her as an opponent. He held no fear for her. To him, this was a fluke, and he would soon regain the upper hand.

JJ had the look of a self-indulgent fitness freak, walking every day in her spandex knee huggers and tank, specially bought *just* for walking in. A lean, *fit* fitness freak who didn't *need* to exercise. She ignored the world, oblivious to all others while she reveled in her morning sweat, listening to her music. She had her own pair of cop-like sunglasses, yes she did, and wore a baseball cap for added shade.

No threat.

Yusev took a right onto West Hadley Road.

The kind of girl who was easy to take. She would never hear him coming, listening to her music cranked up, walking alone at 6:00 a.m. on a quiet Sunday morning on a barren stretch of rural road. By the time she realized what was happening, she would already be lying helpless in the back of his van, her mouth duct-taped shut, her wrists and ankles zip-tied. His victim, whose life was his. The girl who disappeared and was never seen again.

But JJ was no longer that girl.

She thought about it. *Was* she still a girl at all, anymore?

Her free hand drifted to lower abdomen, feeling the dime-sized lump beneath her shirt. The tender, bruised feeling had faded. It had taken about a month to heal. A circle of thick white scar-tissue remained.

She still *looked* like a girl. Same as she always did. For the most part, she felt the same. The one major difference between what she was now and what she used to be was the hunger. And her newest diet.

She didn't want to kill.

She pushed the thoughts away. She needed to concentrate on Yusev. She couldn't afford to have this backfire. She had to use caution, because Yusev *was* experienced. She was a novice. This was only her third time. Her life was on the line, as well as the lives of her future children.

She couldn't allow herself to be distracted by concerns with her recent physical changes.

After a few miles, they came to the village of Hadley. Yusev took the back way to Smith Mountain, along Flash Road.

JJ watched their route carefully. She would know if Yusev deviated.

Yusev turned onto Interstate 81 North. Miles of pavement receded behind the van's rolling tires. He kept the vehicle's speed between 70 and 75 miles an hour in the 65 zone within which they traveled.

She knew everything about him. Every time he had passed her driving by her on her daily walks, she felt a little more of who he was. Through his repeated drives and his thoughts, she had been to his home, his work, and killing room.

THE SHADY SIDE

He lived in a house in the woods in upstate New York, just outside the Adirondack Park. JJ knew the area; she had grown up there.

Yusev's closest neighbors were several miles away. He operated as smartly as he could. He travelled to get his girls. He didn't crap in his own back yard.

He was ideal for JJ's needs.

As the sun rose higher in the summer sky, so did the temperature. Despite having Crannich lower his window and opening her own, as well, the incoming breeze was warm and did nothing to cool the interior of the van. Between the heat and the pain of her hunger, JJ just managed to jerk herself back to awareness before she dozed.

Panicked, JJ's heartbeat kicked up a notch, and she struggled to keep her composure.

"If you have air conditioning, turn it on," she told him. She watched carefully as he pushed a button and dialed the blower to "high".

After a few minutes, JJ was relieved when she began shivering. After about a half hour, the temperature became uncomfortably cold after the sweat dried on her skin, but she welcomed the chill. It would help keep her awake and alert, and hopefully alive.

Yusev had exited the Interstate just past Utica. They were on their way to the foothills.

JJ knew Yusev was planning. She had known that he would. He kept his emotions well in check. He was prepared for the long haul and wasn't worried. After all, they were headed for his home turf. Things would soon change once he entered familiar territory.

Of course, if an opportunity presented itself, he wasn't going to pass it up, either. She hoped that wouldn't happen. Increased stress was JJ's enemy. She couldn't afford to get worked up in a struggle.

But then something else happened that JJ hadn't anticipated, and filled her with dismay.

Three hours into their trip, she felt the slightest urge to urinate.

No, not now!

Their destination was less than an hour away. She could wait.

But as time passed, the slight urge became an urgent need. Having to find a place to stop and relieve herself and then pull it off with Yusev in tow was something she didn't want to contemplate. It would be an opportunity for him to try something.

She didn't want to degrade herself by pissing her spandex knee-huggers. She looked around the back of the van for a bottle, a jar, anything. But there was nothing.

Even if there were, trying to urinate into a container in the moving vehicle while Yusev was driving – no. She would be vulnerable and unable to defend herself.

Then the thought came to her that in little over an hour's time, wet spandex wouldn't matter.

She wasn't that girl anymore, after all.

Her hunger-induced weakness and the call of this stupid human function were going to cause trouble. Her heart rate had doubled again. She needed to restrain herself.

She let go in her spandex.

Just then Yusev glanced into his rearview mirror. "What the *fuck?*" He uttered for the second time that day. JJ read his emotions. *Something's wrong with her face,* they told her. *It looks wrong.*

JJ did a mental check on her face. *Shit.* Her new face was almost showing. Not much; its shadow was just visible beneath her skin. *Damn it, not now!* Her physical issues must have stressed her just enough for some of it to show through.

THE SHADY SIDE

"Shut up!" She said, and gained enough control to shift her face back to normal.

"No, there's something wrong with you!"

"Yeah, there is, my pants are wet. Nature called. Get yourself under control and *drive!*" She didn't want to, but she pulled out her switchblade.

At JJ's revelation, Yusev forgot his fear and began smirking. "Couldn't hold it, huh? What do you think you're doing, anyway? Do you know what you're dealing with?"

"Drive." JJ stuck her blade into the back of Yusev's shoulder and twisted. Her heightened sense of smell quivered at the scent of the fresh warm blood.

"Dammit, *knock it off!* That's gotten really old and *annoying!*" JJ felt his angry resentment bubble up.

Good, she thought. Having Yusev being a little mad was better than having him a lot terrified.

"Then shut. Your mouth. And *drive.*"

He did. But now he was fantasizing even harder about what he was going to do to her when he got home.

* * *

Forty-five minutes later, Yusev turned off the narrow, curving country road onto a pitted and worn dirt track that extended half a mile into the forest. He pulled into the driveway of a neatly maintained clapboard house.

He pushed the gas pedal to the floor, and JJ flew violently backward. She pitched forward again as he slammed his foot on the brake and shifted into park. He reached back and grabbed her ponytail, yanking her head forward and down between the two front seats.

"You stupid bitch! Now you're going to suffer!" He was feeling confident now, her honey-blonde hair gripped in his fist.

Her scalp burned at the base of her ponytail. His grip was so tight that JJ didn't doubt that he might easily pull clumps of hair out of her head.

But pulling JJ's hair was the one thing that could send her into an instant and violent rage.

She bent her wrist and grabbed her switchblade from beneath her wristband. She jammed it into his right side, just below his ribs.

"Ah!" Yusev cried, letting go of her hair.

She pulled herself upright. *"Get out,"* JJ said, clicking off the safety on Yusev's gun. She aimed directly at his head

She climbed into the driver seat after him and nearly landed on top of him when she hopped down out of the van.

She held the gun to his head. He started toward the house.

"No," she said. "The killing room."

"What?" he sounded surprised.

"You dress like a serial killer. You have a serial killer kidnap van and a serial killer hideout. You think like a serial killer. And you act surprised when someone calls you on it? You've killed fifty-four female victims. You planned to do the same to me. You are a murderer and you have a killing room. Take me to it. It isn't in your house."

His confusion was almost painful to feel. He'd been found out. She knew. She knew all about his extracurricular activities. But instead of reporting him to the police, she had turned the tables and kidnapped *him*.

Why?

There was only one answer.

Yusev berated himself for his stupidity. All this time, he hadn't questioned why she had kidnapped *him*. He had only thought of taking control of the situation and having it end as it always did: with a broken woman buried in

THE SHADY SIDE

the ground beneath the trees in his 30-acre back yard. He had never thought for a moment that she might prevail.

With a shout, Yusev turned to run. He ran toward the woods, where his "killing" room was located. A room beneath the roots of decade-old trees. A natural opening into a large cave inside the earth, where no one could ever find it.

He would get there before her. He would lock her out, wait her out, exit through the alternate door.

Except that JJ shot Yusev in the ankle as he broke from her and ran.

"You had to make me go and do that, didn't you? You serial killers are all the same. You have cocky attitudes with delusions of invisibility *and* invincibility. You don't feel fear. That's your first mistake."

The blood ran steadily from Yusev's shattered ankle. It smelled like heaven to JJ, who had been ravenous for a couple of weeks, now. Her last meal had been about a month ago.

At least they lasted a while.

She grabbed Yusev by his ankle and dragged him along the carpet of old, brittle leaves. It was as easy as pulling a homemade scarecrow, like the kind she made for Halloween when she was a child, using dried, dead leaves stuffed in old clothing.

She had gained many gifts from the insect attack. Two of them were increased strength and speed.

Yusev wriggled and squirmed, trying to sit upright as she dragged him between the trees.

Now that JJ was no longer in a vehicle, no longer within the view of the public eye and her mission had nearly been accomplished, she grabbed him by the back of his coverall and tossed him easily over her shoulder. She stretched her sheer lavender wings, then fluttered them until they blurred. She rose from the ground and let loose with all of the conversation she had held back during the ride to Yusev's hideout.

"This is great! You picked an awesome hideout. These trees are so thick that it would be hard to pick me out. It sucks when you can actually fly, but you are afraid to and you know you can't because there are too many people everywhere and they all have cell phones with cameras. Not to mention the drones. They are popular the way kites used to be. A girl can't just go flying any old place without a good chance of getting busted." She navigated between and around the trees, rising to fly over branches, then dropping again to skim the forest floor.

"You know," she continued, "When I was attacked by that giant insect thing, I was *scared*. No, I was *terrified*. And I hurt. A *lot*. The pain was unbearable. But now I feel like a million bucks. I'm a brand-new girl. Yeah," she went on, "I know you don't know what I'm talking about, but it doesn't matter. I can't talk to many people about this." JJ shrugged. "Just you guys – because you aren't around to talk for very long."

She came to a small incline that led down toward the roots of a big old evergreen tree. She dropped Yusev on the ground and pushed him with a barbed black foot. He rolled down the incline and landed against a sturdy wooden door that he had built there, himself.

When he looked at the monster approaching him, he screamed.

It was nearly as big as Yusev. Its body looked like it was covered with pearlescent purple velvet. It had large, translucent wings, tinted a similar purple. The hard, pointed black lips of the thing smiled at him grotesquely from beneath two large, shiny black eyes. Two of its six black, spiky-haired legs waved about in front of it, while it used the two middle and two back legs to walk. As it spoke, the woman's voice coming from the thing's mouth changed from that of a female human to rapid clicking, clacking noises.

Following JJ's earlier example, Yusev pissed in his obvious serial killer custodial coveralls.

JJ kept talking as she climbed over Yusev and splintered the door to his killing room. She grabbed him and pulled him into the space beneath the tree.

"Wow, it really is sooo much cooler down here, isn't it? You know, I don't like killing people. I don't exactly like dining on human flesh, either, especially when it belongs to one of *you* guys." Her insect mouth twisted with distaste as she dragged him down a dark, earthy tunnel.

"Your bodies are filled with toxins that are produced from your nasty thoughts and evil actions." She paused for a moment and contemplated the tunnel ceiling, where tree roots pushed downward through the soil, where thousands of her newly gained, albeit less aggressive and bloodthirsty relatives teemed, busy with their lives' work. "I imagine that a tender young child might taste *so* refreshing. However," she said as she resumed dragging Yusev, who had passed out, "I can't help it. I tried to abstain, you don't know how hard. But obviously, I'm not the same girl anymore, not since the attack."

Here, she came to another sturdy oak door. She pounded at it with her front legs and it splintered as easily as the first door had. She pulled the unconscious Crannich Yusev through it into a large earthen cave. She breathed deeply in relief.

She could finally have her meal... and do the other thing.

"But I figured that if my main diet has to be human, I may as well take out some monsters. That way, I'm not so much a monster, myself. I'm making it possible for who knows how many victims to continue on with their lives. I'm a big hero bug!"

JJ nibbled at Yusev's ankle. "Mmmm," she clicked, "You don't know how long it's been! Thank you so much, Lord, for the feast you have laid upon my table today!" Her wings fluttered happily. She tore voraciously into his leg, making wet, sloppy chomping noises. She smiled, amused.

She looked around the earthen chamber and saw a bloodstained mattress upon a rollaway cot frame, a large table, propane and electric lanterns. A makeshift kitchen area with a cabinet whose door was open to reveal shelves stocked with Sterno and canned goods. Something that looked like a freezer.

And the anguished spirits of many of his victims.

They floated in the dim corners, their eyes drooping exaggeratedly at the corners, their mouths elongated into contorted screams. She could hear them. Their voices sounded faint, as though they originated from many miles away.

A little fixing up, and she could call this home.

"A girl could get used to this. I would be safe here. It's a nice, cool dark place to raise my young. I might stay. But first, there is some cleaning up to do."

JJ didn't eat much from Yusev's calf; just enough to satisfy the worst of her hunger. She had other business to tend to, first. Then she could finish her meal.

Yusev was still passed out. JJ didn't understand how he could just sleep through dinner.

She checked to make sure he was still breathing.

Yup, still alive.

Good.

She used one of her barbed front feet to tear away the front of his serial killer coveralls. Then hooked the same barb into his skin and she tore into that, as well, opening a line from his sternum down to his lower abdomen. She was pulling apart the opening when Yusev came to.

He screamed in terrified agony when he saw what JJ was doing.

"Really?" she clacked. "You brought all of those girls down here and tortured them and killed them, but when it's your turn, you act like a drama queen? You should be honored. You will now be helping to create life, instead of destroying it."

Yusev screamed and screamed. He had lost his cop sunglasses, and even in the dimness, JJ could see his face clearly. His ice-blue eyes fairly glowed with terror. The rest of his bristly face was that of an old, gray man.

"Dammit, *knock it off!* That's gotten really old and *annoying!*" JJ mocked him. "You are harshing on my mellow. Destroying my Zen." She bent over his throat and clipped it with her sharp black lips. His scream cut off abruptly. She took his head in her mouth, shook it until it came loose, and tossed it aside.

"That's better," JJ clicked.

Yusev's head came to rest with his face toward JJ. His eyes were open. The last thing he saw before he died was a giant insect squatting over his body, depositing a cache of eggs into his abdomen among his still-warm entrails and organs.

The screams of his victims rose into a shrill cacophony as they swirled together, and in a misty cloud, they streamed out the door, up the earthen tunnel, and out into the open air, where their incorporeal forms pulled apart and dissipated into long awaited freedom.

AUGUST

Charles Gantlen guided his car slowly down the rural road. The autumn afternoon sunshine slanted between the bordering trees, creating bars of light and dark across the unlined pavement. The thick expanse of evergreens gave off a pleasant Christmassy scent in the warm, gentle breeze.

There. There she was. A slender young woman in black spandex and a purple tank shirt. Long, dark blonde hair in a thick ponytail that cascaded down between her shoulder blades. Short white socks, white sneakers. Black wires led from bright neon green earbuds down to her mp3 player hooked onto her waistband.

Oblivious to everything, listening to music, looking at her cell phone.

She was there, speed walking, every day at the same time, her supple arms and legs muscular and tan.

The road was empty for miles in both directions.

Gantlen slowed and considered, grinning to himself.

Maybe today would be the day.

WRATH

August, 1996

The murder gathered in the trees beside the Wamalak River about two hours before the storm ravaged Gridley County. They chose the most densely wooded areas on the south side of the German Street Bridge. Their leader knew that the more thickly wooded their retreat, the greater their protection against the devastating storm winds that fast approached from the southwest. The crows numbered roughly 600; of these, 111 were chicks less than six months old.

The cacophony of their impromptu meeting echoed for a radius of at least a half mile from their shelter, but most of the residents of Smith Mountain that lived nearby took no notice. They were either at work or out of town on day trips or vacations, savoring the remaining days of their dwindling summer.

When the crows' uproar suddenly died down, no one noticed that, either. All of nature in Gridley County quieted beneath the flaming yellow sun and robin's egg blue sky. The day fell into a lazy tranquility.

Within the next half hour, the sky darkened with a mass of dark blue and purple storm clouds. Lightning flashed in the distant hills. The wind picked up, blowing through the city streets and country lanes. It tossed people's garbage cans around, picked up lawn chairs and flung them into the street, ripped up tent moorings, and threw potted plants around easily, as though they were made of tissue.

As the first fat raindrops fell, people scurried outside to roll up their car windows, and those who were out and about hurried to get to shelter. Over at Orange Beach, the on-duty lifeguards ordered all swimmers out of the water, and picnickers in the pavilions packed up their coolers, doused their barbeques, and headed home.

Lighting forked without respite across the heavens, leaving fading jagged white streaks against a yellow-green sky. It was so bright, close and widespread that it caused a momentary freeze-frame effect every time it flashed. Warm and cold air banks clashed high above, and booming thunder vibrated across the earth.

The furious gale bent the more flexible trees sideways, their tops parallel with the ground. It ripped those with larger, stiffer trunks out of the ground by their roots, dropping them onto houses and cars whose roofs caved in like so much wet cardboard. Utility poles fell across the rapidly flooding streets. Bicycles, outdoor toys, picnic tables, and all manner of yard items sailed across town, landing in the streets and in unfamiliar neighborhoods. Several of the small private aircraft in storage on the tarmac at the airport rolled end over end, the wings breaking off in pieces.

The crows held on for dear life in the trees near the river, but not all of them could withstand the fury of the storm. Over 150 mature corvids suffered injuries, and 37 were killed. Of the 111 chicks, 66 survived; and 21 of the survivors were injured.

* * *

At Eleven Laurel Avenue, Paisley Jones, novelist, flower child, and birder and lover of all things nature opened her front door with caution and poked her head outside. She inhaled sharply at her first view of the devastation yesterday's storm had wrought upon her neighborhood.

Trash cans and flower pots littered her yard. A large tree branch had smashed through the windshield of the truck that belonged to Jacob Porter, the elderly gentleman who lived across the street. A red tricycle lay in the middle of Laurel Avenue, its metal handlebars twisted nearly beyond recognition. Beside it lay some of the slats from her friend and neighbor Marjorie's wooden fence; more slats lay haphazardly in other residents' yards. Paisley's bird feeders had been tossed carelessly into the tree line beside her house, and her lawn chairs lay in the nearby intersection.

Many of her neighbors were already outside, helping one another with their clean-up efforts.

As Paisley bent to gather up her flowerpots, she spied a tiny black crow lying beneath some broken branches. At first she thought the chick was dead, but as she kneeled to examine the bird, she saw that it was trying to lift its head. One of its eyes looked injured; it was closed and crusted over.

Through its one good eye, it vaguely saw Paisley Jones as a pair of large brown eyes in a sea of white framed by thick, dark brown dreadlocks, all of which was surrounded by a nimbus of yellow light. The spicy scent of patchouli wafted from her brightly patterned rust-and-brown colored tunic. The chick opened his beak feebly, emitting a tiny squawk.

"Oh, you poor baby!" Paisley exclaimed.

She ran into her house and looked around desperately for something to transport the baby crow in. She found a picnic basket in her closet. She set it on the floor and dumped some of her guinea pig's timothy hay in the bottom.

She grabbed the basket and her widest cooking spatula from the kitchen and ran outside. Squatting, she slid the plastic spatula beneath the crow chick. She lifted it carefully and laid it on the green hay in the bottom of the basket, slipping the spatula from beneath the small feathered body. Her white face and large brown eyes were the last thing the young corvid saw before Paisley lowered the lid and darkness enclosed him.

Paisley set the basket on the front seat of her car and scoured her small front yard, looking for any other feathered or mammalian casualties of the storm that she might have missed.

Finding no more injured creatures, she grabbed her purse, locked her house, and drove the chick to the Kingfisher Wildlife Health Center in Toulaine County.

It was slow going. A normal drive out of the city usually took only ten or fifteen minutes, maybe twenty minutes during rush hour. The drive out of town this morning took forty-five.

Though clean-up crews and the residents of Smith Mountain were out in force, picking up debris, downed trees and telephone wires, the streets were still a mess. Many were closed to traffic, and police were everywhere, diverting traffic around hazards, and Paisley was re-routed several times.

Paisley found that the outskirts of Smith Mountain were in better shape; and once she crossed the county line, she saw that Toulaine County had been virtually untouched by the storm.

THE SHADY SIDE

One of the staff at the Wildlife Health Center asked Paisley a few questions and gave her a form to fill out. He looked the chick over briefly and admitted it for treatment. When he saw the small, brown-eyed woman looking anxiously at the basket, he smiled kindly.

"There's a box on the form that you can check if you would like us to contact you to let you know how the chick is doing. Just fill out your name and phone number."

Paisley thanked him and finished filling out the form. When she handed it back to the staff member, she noticed the strange look he gave her. At first she thought it was because of her dreads; then he snapped his fingers and smiled.

"*Yoga Recipes*, right?"

Paisley smiled. "Yes, that's right."

"I loved your book! The title really threw me off guard. I am not much of a genre reader, but your book surprised me. When is your next one coming out?"

"Oh, I'm working on it," Paisley responded vaguely. "I really hope you can help him," she said, changing the subject.

"I'm sorry? Oh, yes, the crow! He doesn't seem to be too bad. But we will see. One of us will contact you as soon as we know."

"Thank you!" With a last worried glance toward the door through which the crow had been taken, she exited the Wildlife Health Center and went back home.

Two days later, the staff called Paisley to let her know that the chick would survive, and that after his initial treatment, he would be fostered in the home of a wildlife rehabilitation professional. The chick was eventually placed in the care of the Kingfisher Ornithology Clinic.

May, 1997

"We've loved having you here, Einstein, but I think it's high time you all experience the wide world," Dr. Nancy Grant said.

"*Love you,*" squawked Einstein, cocking his head to look at the doctor out of his one good eye.

"See, we've hooked you up with some fancy bling," Dr. Grant said.

"*Bling,*" said Einstein. "*Ninety-nine!*"

"That's right," said the doctor. "Ninety-nine is an awesome number for a genius bird like you." She scratched the corvid's feathered head as he leaned in.

Later that day, the staff released Einstein 99 and Nikola 67, a fellow victim of the previous year's summer storm. Each of them was outfitted with a square white wing-tag which bore their respective numbers in big black print, as well as a matching numbered leg band.

Several of the staff gathered outside to see the crows off on their journey. They waved and called, "We love you guys! We'll miss you!" and, "Be safe! Happy travels!"

The two corvids could not have asked for a better day to fly. The early May sky was crisp and clear, and the birds wheeled, dived, and sailed along on the gentle air currents.

Einstein took the lead, flying the nineteen miles back to the neat white Cape Cod at Eleven Laurel Avenue in the City of Smith Mountain.

The two half-grown crows perched on Paisley's porch railing and greeted her when opened her front door that afternoon.

"Holy crow!" she exclaimed, smiling broadly.

Thereafter, they remained in the vicinity of her house, often found roosting in the adjacent tree line, visiting on her porch, or communing with various species of fellow birds in her yard. The two crows and the female human became fast friends.

The corvids had no reason to travel far, or to dig into the garbage bags on Tuesdays. On garbage day, Paisley often tossed leftover fruits into her front yard; and the nearby farms were near busy roads, where pickings were plentiful.

March, 1998

Einstein 99 sat atop his favorite utility pole. He fluffed out his feathers against the damp chill. The warming temperatures and late March rains had melted the remaining snow mounds, leaving only thin patches of white crust here and there atop the sodden green grass that covered the slowly thawing soil. A swift blanket of churning cloud cover roiled overhead in tattered, cottony gray puffs and streams, filtering daybreak's pale light.

Between five and eight o'clock a.m., Laurel Avenue and the surrounding neighborhood slowly awakened. Various residents emerged from their homes to walk their dogs. Children gathered on sidewalk corners, waiting for the school bus. Cars, trucks, SUVs, and minivans idled in driveways, warming up in readiness to convey their owners to work.

Einstein scanned the houses and streets below.

Paisley came out of her front door, her leashed pug dog, Gargoyle, trotting out ahead of her. Next door to Paisley's house, Marjorie Thorpe (the Orange Car Lady and Paisley's good friend), carried her blue City of Smith Mountain trash bag out to the curb, where it joined the other fat blue bags of trash that lined the curbs on either side of the street.

Across the street, Jacob Porter (the Old Guy) let his old basset hound out into his fenced-in back yard.

Einstein watched the street with a sharp, black eye. The large crow stretched his damp wings restlessly, the square white lab tags with the black number "99" staying firmly affixed to the glistening black feathers.

After a few minutes, Paisley came back with Gargoyle. They disappeared inside the house.

Einstein was gratified when the red front door of the white Cape Cod opened once more and Paisley stepped out onto the porch. She tossed out five apples and broke up several slices of white bread into small pieces, scattering them on top of the grass.

Einstein flew down to greet her. "*Paisey!*"

She scratched him briefly on top of his feathered head.

Nikola sailed down from the bordering tree line. The crows were still snatching up pieces of bread when Paisley emerged from her house one last time, to leave for work.

"Goodbye, guys!" she waved to them as she pulled out of her driveway.

Around nine o'clock, the morning bustle of human activity stilled and the unseen daily lives of the birds and four-legged creatures carried on as usual.

Bluebell, the Orange Car Lady's indoor-outdoor cat, squeezed out of an opening in the door of Paisley's shed. Her two-week old kitten, Jasmine, dangled from her mouth. She trotted down the driveway and slipped into a hole in the lattice skirting surrounding the Orange Car Lady's porch.

Squirrels chattered from dripping tree branches. A variety of neighborhood birds ignored the rain in favor of flocking on and around the various feeding stations that dotted the human residents' yards.

Einstein and Nikola were digging into the apples, gulping down the sweet, soft pulp, when Einstein sensed a new presence. He paused and looked up. The Stranger who lived at Six Laurel Avenue was standing on his front porch, looking around, up and down the street.

Einstein eyed the human cautiously before putting one clawed foot on top of his apple, holding it in place as he resumed devouring his breakfast. He kept his suspicious eye on the Stranger as the big man descended his front steps and headed down the sidewalk in the crow's direction.

The Stranger had arrived in the neighborhood three weeks before, moving into the small brown ranch house down the street that had sat empty for nearly a year. Einstein didn't know the human well; he had rarely seen the man. Einstein had an idea that the Stranger's work hours were somewhat odd when compared with the average schedule the rest of the neighborhood followed. From what the sharp-eyed corvid had seen, the Stranger was usually gone by four o'clock in the morning, well before the rest of the residents began to stir. He generally pulled back into his driveway in the afternoon between one and three o'clock. Beyond that, Einstein 99 knew very little of Laurel Avenue's newest addition.

The bird didn't trust the Stranger's aura, though. While the residents of Laurel Avenue possessed a colorful rainbow of auras, the muddy nimbus that surrounded the Stranger was shot through with dark red streaks. It didn't seem natural, and it made Einstein feel uneasy.

The corvid paused in his meal again as he watched the Stranger swagger down the driveway beside the house, ignoring the crows on the lawn.

Curious, Einstein abandoned his apple and flew up to the top of the wooden fence that separated Paisley's driveway from the Orange Car Lady's driveway next door.

The Stranger was dressed in attire that Einstein had never seen him wear before: He wore a standard blue uniform shirt with a rectangular name tag sewn above the left breast pocket, dark blue pants, and a white hardhat that covered his strawberry-blonde hair. He carried a clipboard in one hand and a pen in the other. He looked like any of the utility workers that Einstein periodically saw on the block.

The corvid fluttered briefly to the rear of the house and perched on a tree branch as the man mounted the back steps. He removed what seemed to be a stiff card from beneath the large metal clip on the clipboard. He cast a furtive glance around before leaning over the doorknob. A few seconds later, the door swung open, and the Stranger entered the house, pulling the door closed behind him.

Einstein called to Nikola. They flew to the tree line that separated Paisley's house from the neighbor's residence on the west side. Einstein tilted his head, focusing his beady black eye on Paisley's windows. Their interiors were hung with sheer curtains, which blocked a clear view into the house. But from this vantage point, Einstein's sharp eye could discern the Stranger's dark shadow behind the curtains and was able follow his movement through the first floor of the house.

A while later, Einstein saw the Stranger's dark silhouette move toward the back door. After a moment, the man emerged and walked down the driveway to the sidewalk. He scanned the street and neighboring houses. Seeing no one, he hurried across the street and down the sidewalk to his own house.

Einstein knew the six-block area of this neighborhood well. He knew which humans lived in each house, and he was familiar with all of the regular visitors that came and went – including the mail carrier and the various utility workers that came from the gas and electric companies.

The Stranger was different. Though he dressed the part that morning, Einstein didn't believe he was a utility worker. They usually went to every house on the street, not just to one.

Einstein had never seen the Stranger with Paisley. His instincts told him that the Stranger did not belong inside Paisley's home, and that Paisley didn't know about the Stranger's visit. The big black crow didn't like the human's furtive air, the smell of underhandedness that came off him in waves, and his dark and dirty aura.

Einstein was sure that the Stranger was a threat to Paisley.

* * *

The Stranger showed up again a few days later, wearing his utility worker costume. Einstein and his associates watched him warily.

The corvid leader flew up to the top of the shed at the end of the driveway beside the back yard. From there, he could see the Stranger from the side as he approached the back door and had a better view of what the Stranger was doing than when he had previously observed the human from the backyard tree.

He tipped his head sideways and watched the Stranger remove the card from the clipboard. It appeared to be a credit card. He slid it between the door frame and the metal latch. In a second, the back door was open and the Stranger slipped inside.

Einstein had seen all he needed to confirm his suspicions.

He knew how locks worked. Everyone he had ever seen enter a locked residence had used their shiny metal keys. Einstein 99 was, in fact, guilty of pilfering such keys on multiple occasions, causing different human neighborhood inhabitants varying degrees of consternation when they found themselves locked out of their homes.

Humans used metal keys to open the locks on their doors. They did *not* use credit cards.

If the Stranger had been welcome in Paisley's domicile while she was away, she would have provided the Stranger with a key of his own, or would have shown the Stranger where the spare key was hidden.

Now, Einstein was sure that this human was shady. Paisley was unaware of the Stranger's most likely unwelcome presence in her home.

"*Cawcawcaw!*" Einstein took off and flew back to the tree line, as he had the first time the Stranger had trespassed into Paisley's home. He and Nikola usually roosted there at night, as Paisley's bedroom was located on the second floor of that side of the house. She often opened her curtains so that she could see the trees and let the light into her room. The curtains were wide open, today. Einstein perched on a branch outside the window.

The Stranger was inside Paisley's bedroom. Einstein watched him rifle through the drawers in Paisley's dresser. He then turned his attention to the bookshelves, examining the titles on the book spines, pulling out a book here and there and leafing through it.

He eventually made his way to the bedside table, where Paisley kept a large box that she locked with a combination padlock. He pulled something thin and shiny out of his pocket and used it to fiddle with the lock. In a few seconds, the lock opened, and the Stranger removed it from the box. He sat on the bed and opened the lid. He pulled out a spiral-bound notebook with a black cover.

He sat and read through the black-covered notebook for a while, turning page after page. He pulled out his cell phone and took pictures of some of the pages.

Eventually, the Stranger returned the notebook to the box and locked it. He left the room.

THE SHADY SIDE

Einstein flew to the front lawn pecked at the remains of that morning's apple. He saw the Stranger open the curtains and check to make sure no one was around outside. A moment later, he left the house and crossed the street. When he reached his car, he folded himself into the driver's seat and started it. He began backing out of the driveway.

"*Caw! Cawcawcaw!*" Einstein launched himself into the air, calling to his associates. Nikola flew up behind him, accompanied by six more crows of the murder.

They stayed high above and behind the Stranger's car as he drove through the city. Though he increased his speed when he hit Smith Mountain's outskirts, the crows' height enabled them to see many miles ahead. They also had the advantage of being able to keep to one direction and just alter slightly when the car made a turn or went around a curve.

The mild weather made it an easy flight.

When the car turned onto a heavily wooded road in Frond, a town in the neighboring Toulaine County, the eight crows descended, skimming the treetops, keeping sight of the car through the ripe green foliage. Eventually the vehicle slowed and turned right onto a wooded drive marked only by a couple of grassy tracks. The crows dispersed among the branches, flitting silently from tree to tree.

Deep in the woods, the air was cooler and tinted green by the sunlight filtered through the leaves. The tranquility was only disturbed by the chirps and calls of feathered residents and the shuffling of small animals through the leaves and brush.

A slight squeak of the car's brakes signaled its halt. Einstein 99 peered down from his perch and saw the Stranger had parked his shiny black car next to a freshly dug hole about three feet deep; a spade was stuck upright in the pile of dirt that sat beside the earthy opening.

The Stranger shut off his car and got out. The thick foliage of the surrounding trees muffled the sound of his car door closing. He set off in a diagonal direction; Einstein's sharp eye saw that the man was following a well-worn animal path that wound between the trees.

Einstein and the other crows sailed down and tailed him, barely rustling the branches as they hopped from tree to tree.

The Stranger eventually paused, standing behind a tree, leaning around it and focusing on the house in the large, circular clearing that lay before him. After about five minutes he stepped out from behind the tree and approached the house.

Einstein and his associates alighted in the tall pines that surrounded the house at the very edge of the clearing. The corvid leader tipped his head sideways, observing with his bright black eye as the Stranger approached the front door. The Stranger pulled a card from his wallet and used it to compromise the lock; the same trick he had used to gain entrance to Paisley's house.

The curtains in this house were opened wide in every window around the house, so the crows were able to track the Stranger's movements from the perches they had chosen among the deciduous trees that dotted the yard. He moved from room to room, pausing often for several minutes before moving on. He didn't seem to be doing much except looking through the absent inhabitant's belongings.

Eventually, the Stranger looked out the front window, checking the front yard and the driveway. He came out the front door a moment later, pulling it closed behind him. He whistled jauntily as he headed down the wooded path back to his car.

***

THE SHADY SIDE

The Stranger returned at least once each week, sometimes more often. His pattern was consistent. He would slip into the back door of Paisley's house. He would remain inside for some time, usually less than an hour. He would then emerge from the house and leave just as quietly as he came.

Einstein watched what he could through Paisley's windows. He was uncomfortable with the human going through Paisley's belongings; he knew it was wrong. But the Stranger never seemed to remove anything from the home or disturb anything that Einstein could see. He came and went without incident. He was oblivious to the crows; to him, they were just birds.

Einstein kept a vigilant eye on the intruder, regardless. The dark, smoky light that reflected from his person told the corvid leader that even though he hadn't harmed Paisley – yet – he was dangerous, and there would be trouble. Einstein felt it in his gut.

He and a group of his associates often followed the man when he left his little brown ranch house. They tailed him to his workplace, to the grocery store, to what Einstein assumed were the homes of nearby friends and relatives; everywhere the Stranger went, Einstein and his associates followed.

They tailed him to the house in the Frond woods on several occasions. On every trip, the Stranger's behavior echoed the behavior he exhibited at Paisley's house: wearing some kind of disguise that helped him look legit, he would sneak in, spend time inside the home, then walk out.

The one difference between the Stranger's visits to Paisley's house and the house in the woods was that when the Stranger ended his visits to the house in the woods, he finished by digging.

The small hole that the crows had seen when they first tailed the Stranger to the Frond woods had grown, as had the pile of dark, moist earth beside it. The hole was now several feet deep and had taken on a rectangular shape, about three feet wide and six feet long.

Einstein 99 and some of his associates had had the opportunity to observe more than one funeral. They would sit atop the taller monuments in the cemetery or perch in the high branches above the service and watch the solemn groups of people dressed in the customary black clothing. Einstein had seen open graves, had observed as polished caskets were slowly lowered down into these earthy holes.

The large hole in the woods closely resembled a cemetery grave.

The Stranger had finished one grave and begun digging a second.

July, 1998

A torrential afternoon downpour dwindled to a warm drizzle, and Einstein and Nikola huddled together and dozed, hidden among the early summer's full, ripe foliage in the tree line beside Paisley's house.

Einstein heard footsteps sloshing through the puddles on the wet sidewalk. He opened his good eye and turned his head. He straightened up when he saw the Stranger approaching, wearing his customary hard hat and utility uniform disguise. The corvid leader stayed where he was, sandwiched between Nikola and the trunk of the tree where they were nestled. His current perch was his regular night-time roost, right outside her bedroom window.

True to form, the Stranger let himself into Paisley's room. Einstein watched lazily while the intruder leafed through her journals. Eventually a faint noise broke Einstein's concentration, distracting him.

THE SHADY SIDE

Curious as to the source of the sound, Einstein stretched his wings and glided down from his branch into the front yard. He couldn't see anything in the immediate vicinity, so he stood still and listened for a moment. The noise seemed to be coming from the other side of the house, where the driveway was located. He cawed briefly and strutted around the corner of the house. There, in the driveway, sat Jasmine, Bluebell's sodden gray and white kitten, meowing and crying for her mother.

Bluebell got along well with the crows; they were friends of a sort, so Einstein and his associates looked out for Bluebell and her kitten.

As the big crow hopped over to Jasmine to offer some comfort, the Stranger came around the back corner of Paisley's house. He saw the crow and the kitten in the middle of the driveway. Spying a big puddle nearby, he walked over to it and kicked the murky water, splashing the bird and the young feline.

"Caw!" Einstein flapped his wings at the Stranger. *"Stop!"* he squawked one of the many words he had learned from the staff at the Kingfisher Lab.

The Stranger raised his thick, light-colored eyebrows. "*Stop*, huh? You're a smart bird, aren't you?" He paused and leaned over, looking at the tag on the corvid's wing. "*Ninety-nine*. You can talk? You must be a genius." His eyes were large and sea-green, glowing brightly out of his tan, weathered face. His nostrils flared, broadening his already wide nose, making it look much bigger than it was. His thin lips curled up derisively. "Well, watch this."

Before Einstein knew what was happening, the Stranger swung his sneakered foot and connected with Jasmine's soft underbelly. The kitten yowled in pained surprise as her small body flew across the pavement into the Orange Car Lady's front yard.

"Cawcawcawcaw!" Einstein called, his voice loud in the quiet afternoon. Nikola and several other associates flew down from their afternoon roost.

Einstein flew at the Stranger, flapping his wings. The other crows swooped down as the Stranger tried to escape across the street. Einstein struck the Stranger's head with his wings and rapped his beak against the man's skull as hard as he could, while his associates harried him, taking jabs at his neck, pinching his arms, pulling his hair, and grabbing any part of him that they could get to.

The Stranger shouted out and waved his arms, trying to hit at and deflect the flurry of big black wings, sharp talons, and rock-hard beaks. His defensive efforts failing, the Stranger wrapped his arms around his head protectively and ran down the sidewalk to his house, the crows surrounding him like a small black cloud, alive with shiny black feathers.

After the Stranger had escaped into his house, the crows flew back to Jasmine. By then, Bluebell had returned and was comforting her offspring. The Stranger's vicious kick hadn't seriously injured the kitten; nevertheless, Bluebell moved her to secluded safety until the Orange Car Lady returned home from work.

Einstein sat atop the utility pole for the next couple of hours, watching and waiting; but the Stranger did not emerge from his home again until well after dark. By then the entire murder were settled into their roost for the night.

The corvid leader kept watch over the Stranger for the next several days, but the human did not make his way across the street for three weeks. In fact, the Stranger's prolonged absence lulled Einstein 99 into believing that he wouldn't be back again.

THE SHADY SIDE

* * *

When the Stranger emerged from his house and made his way across the street one Tuesday morning, Einstein was breakfasting at a neighborhood feeder three streets away. He had no inkling of trouble until he heard a commotion and Nikola 67 cawing urgently: *"Stranger! Stranger!"*

Einstein left his meal and took off toward Laurel Avenue. He alighted on his favorite utility pole and scanned the street and houses below. The deserted street seemed serene.

He heard a volley of crow calls from several of his associates and flew toward their voices, which emanated from the tree line beside the Paisley's house. As he sailed over her yard, he sighted the Stranger, who crouched in a small opening between the trees. He was sighting along the length of an air rifle which he aimed toward the sky.

Crack! The sudden sound echoed between the houses. Einstein felt the rush of air as a tiny projectile zinged past him. He changed course and flew to the protective cover of the nearby treetops.

"Back!" He called the warning to all of his associates. He heard an answering caw and saw Nikola 67's outspread wings silhouetted against the blue sky.

The Stranger pumped the air rifle. He took careful aim at Nikola.

Crack! The sleek black corvid plummeted down onto the Old Guy's lawn across the street. She lay still, a dark shadow against the ripe, green grass.

The Stranger looked up, searching through the trees, and spied Einstein 99. He shook the air rifle at the crow. "Oops! I got the wrong one!" he laughed triumphantly.

He looked around to make sure the neighborhood was still deserted; then he ran across the street to the fallen crow. He took a pair of wire cutters from his pocket and cut the white tags away from Nikola's wings. Then he removed both metal ankle bracelets. "There," he said. "Now you're just another mangy crow in the crowd."

Then he headed back across the street toward his house.

Followed by the rest of his associates, Einstein 99 flew down to his fallen brother. He contemplated Nikola's lifeless body, how it lay as if carelessly thrown there, the wings haphazardly arranged, the black beak open, as were Nikola's eyes. The glorious deep midnight blue that had once reflected from his feathers had grown dull.

Einstein felt a poisonous emotion bubble up through his feathered breast.

He stared balefully toward the Stranger's car, which was just disappearing around the corner.

"Caw! Cawcawcaw!" Einstein called out instructions for one of the elder crows to oversee the murder's viewing of their deceased associate.

As a group of crows gathered around Nikola, Einstein and his closest eight associates launched in pursuit of the Stranger.

He led them back to the house in the Frond woods.

He exited his shiny black car. Holding a paper folder in his hands, he stood at the edge of one of the finished graves, looking down inside, nodding in satisfaction.

He opened the folder and took something out; a small, square piece of paper. To Einstein, it looked like a photograph. The Stranger gazed at the image on the paper for a moment, then smiled, kissed it, and tossed it into the grave. He walked slowly to the side of the second grave and repeated the kiss on another square of paper, again tossing the square into the grave, where it floated gently down to the hole's earthy floor.

Before following the Stranger down the animal path to the house in the clearing, Einstein sailed down into one of the graves. Curious about the squares of paper, he

THE SHADY SIDE

wanted to take a look. The first square was a photo of a pretty young blonde woman.

Einstein flitted up out of the hole and to the bottom of the second grave, where the photo lay face down. He used one claw tip to flip the paper over.

The face in this photo belonged to Paisley Jones.

"Paisey! Paisey!" Einstein cawed frantically. He flew up out of the grave, his associates joining him in his mad flight to the house in the clearing.

The crows reached their perches in time to see the front door close behind the Stranger as he entered the house. Einstein cawed softly, and he and his associates settled in to wait.

Soon, they heard the sound of an approaching vehicle, and watched as a light blue car pulled into the long driveway. Einstein's heart sank as when he saw that the car was driven by the blonde woman he had seen in the photo. The overhead garage door rose and the car disappeared inside, the door slowly lowering behind it, cutting off the view.

The temperature was beginning to drop in tandem with the sun's descent through the sky, which had filled with an array of cottony white clouds that moved swiftly across the blue expanse. Borne by the late afternoon breeze, they created massive shadows moved across the square brown and green fields of the farmlands that lay adjacent to the woods.

Einstein puffed up his feathers against the coming chill and settled against the sturdy gray trunk of the young maple tree he had chosen as his perch.

A few moments had passed when the feathered observers heard loud thumping noises coming from the inside of the house, and then a scream.

Soon, the Stranger peered out the window, checking the yard and driveway.

The front door opened. The Stranger emerged onto the porch. His usual smoky aura was now pulsing a rusty, brick red shade. He carried something large in a black bag which he held draped over his right shoulder. He pulled the door closed firmly behind him and strode across the porch, descended the steps and cut across the bright green lawn, returning to the animal path that would lead him back to his car.

Hot on the Stranger's tail, Einstein saw something white protruding from the opening in the bag that hung down the Stranger's back. He dropped down to a lower branch as surreptitiously as he could.

Finally, he was close enough to the bag to recognize what dangled limply from the opening. There were two of them. They were a pair of human feet clad in white sneakers.

The Stranger was carrying a human in the black bag. Einstein thought it had to be the woman who had driven into the garage in the light blue car: the blonde woman from the photograph.

The man reached the place in the woods where he had parked his car. He tossed the black bag into the grave where the blonde woman's photo lay. The bag landed with a thud.

A woman's voice cried out, the thin sound carrying weakly out of the rectangular opening and up through the trees.

The Stranger pulled the spade from its resting place in the corner of the grave. He dug into the pile of dirt beside the grave, pulling the moist brown earth toward him, over the edge and into the hole. It sprayed across the top of the bag, making a sound like rain falling on plastic, or on top of a car's roof.

The woman's voice cried out again, this time a little louder.

"Help! Help me!"

THE SHADY SIDE

Einstein sat up straight on his perch, realizing now exactly what was happening.

The Stranger was a rogue human. He was going to kill the woman and bury her.

The man threw the shovel down into the hole. He turned around backward and positioned himself to climb down a ladder that Einstein hadn't seen before because its dark frame blended in with the shadows of the hole in which it rested.

Einstein glided to the edge of the hole and peered down. He saw the Stranger heft the spade and raise it over his head. He brought it down hard onto the closed end of the bag. A scream of pain emanated from the bag and drifted up from the hole.

"Caw! Cawcawcaw!" Einstein called urgently, and dropped down onto the Stranger's shoulder. He pecked at the human's eyes and pulled at his hair and eyelids.

Answering his call, his associates flew down into the grave and bombarded the Stranger like sleek, feathered projectiles.

He stumbled as their vicious beaks pounded at his skull, leaving dull, aching pain and numb white-hot spots where they struck him. One of their beaks gripped his right ear, pulling it and ripping it from its place on the side of his head as he screamed. A wide strip of the skin in front of his ear tore off deep into his cheek. The tip of another beak dug into the softness of the Stranger's eye, which offered no resistance as it was simply scooped of the socket and the attached bloody strings severed with one snap. Still others gripped clumps of his hair and pulled so hard that pieces of his scalp came away with it.

The black bag shifted and moved as the woman inside it pushed against the plastic, the Stranger's tortured screams sending her deeper into panic. She wriggled and squirmed, finally pushing it off of her head. It fell to the earth, revealing the bright red blood that ran in streams from the wounds in her scalp, streaking down her blonde hair and splashing brilliantly against her white button-down shirt.

She screamed when she saw the flurry of black wings filling the air around her. The nine crows barely all fit into the grave together with her assailant, who had stopped screaming. Now there were only the sounds of flapping wings, their impact against the man's body and ripping noises as their beaks tore at his skin, hair and clothing.

He fell to his knees and the blonde woman crouched with her face against the earth in one corner of the grave, her arms curled protectively around her head.

"Stop! Stop! Pretty lady, pretty lady!" Einstein called. His associates immediately ceased their attack, backing off and flapping up to the edges of the hole. The Stranger fell forward onto his face, pieces of his scalp hanging from his skull, strips of his skin and shirt likewise hanging from his body in a macabre, tattered fringe. Bloody tears from his empty eye sockets streaked his face and mixed with the dirt upon which his cheek now rested.

The terrified woman screamed and cried in the corner of the grave.

"Please don't hurt me! Please don't hurt me!" she sobbed.

"Caw!" Einstein hopped over to her and regarded her quietly until she stopped screaming. Hearing nothing but silence around her, her body still hitching with sobs, she lowered one of her arms and peered over her shoulder.

She saw her assailant lying still and the big crow sitting beside her, regarding her sharply out of his one good eye.

"Einstein help! Pretty lady!" he said.

The woman noticed his tagged wings and banded leg.

"Help pretty lady!" he repeated.

THE SHADY SIDE

The woman looked up and saw the other eight crows perched around the edge of the grave, looking down at her.

"Out!" Einstein hopped and strutted awkwardly to the end of the grave where the ladder stood waiting.

"Oh my God, yes!" The woman scrambled out of her corner and stumbled to the ladder. Einstein flew to the edge of the grave and waited for her to reach the top. She flopped out onto the soft grass beside the edge of the hole.

She sat up and looked at the nine crows who silently surrounded her. She started crying tears of relief. "Can you tell me what direction home is in?"

Grateful to receive a positive response from the traumatized woman, Einstein shouted, *"Home!"* He flapped his wings, flying up to a nearby branch.

The woman rose to her feet and followed, escorted by the nine corvids.

When they reached her house in the clearing, she ran up the steps to her door. But before she ran inside to call for help, she turned to the crows now perched on her railing and in the trees dotted throughout her yard.

"Thank you!" She sobbed.

"Welcome!" Einstein responded.

He and his associates flew back to Paisley's house.

* * *

The high-pitched wail of sirens pierced the dusk. Paisley Jones, enjoying a Friday evening glass of wine with Marjorie on her porch, watched as five police cars pulled up into the driveway and parked in the street in front of number Six Laurel Avenue.

Her neighbors emerged from their homes, watching as the uniformed officers pounded on the door of the brown ranch house, then unceremoniously kicked in the door, guns drawn.

"Wow!" Marjorie exclaimed. "What do you think is going on?"

Paisley shrugged and sipped her wine. "Damned if *I* know," she responded.

A sixth police car pulled up in front of number Eleven, Paisley's own home.

"Holy shit, Pais, they're coming *here!*" Marjorie said.

"What the hell?" Paisley murmured as two uniformed officers exited the car. Paisley sat unmoving, a chill invading her chest.

"Are you Paisley Jones?"

"I am," she said.

"Do you know a man named Jory Folkner?"

Paisley shook her head. "The name isn't familiar to me. I don't think I've ever heard it before."

One of the officers held out a photograph. "Do you recognize this man?"

"Why yes. He lives down the street. In the brown house." Her brow furrowed as she looked down the street toward the commotion coming from the brown ranch house. "Why? What's going on?"

"We have reason to believe that you have been a potential target of this man."

Marjorie gasped, her eyes wide.

"*What?* Are you *kidding* me?" Paisley said.

"We know that this will most likely come as a shock to you, Miss Jones. But could you please spare a few moments to come to the station with us? We would like to ask you a few questions and take a statement."

"About what?"

"About any kind of contact you may have had with this man. And we have questions about some crows that we believe you know."

"You mean *Einstein?*"

The officer sighed. "We know that this is all very sudden. But we think you may be able to fill in some

THE SHADY SIDE

missing pieces of a puzzle. Would you please come to the station and talk to us? You aren't under arrest or a suspect. We just need as much information as we can get. And there is something you need to see."

"I've been drinking. I can't drive."

"We'll give you a ride."

"Marjorie. You haven't touched a drop, yet. Will you take me?"

"You betcha, Pais. I wouldn't miss this!"

At the station, Marjorie sat in a chair in the hallway outside the Detective's office.

Paisley sat in the chair opposite the detective's desk.

"I'm Detective Leon," he said, glancing at her. "It is nice to meet you, Miss... Paisley *Jones?*" he looked at her face again. "Wow, *Yoga Recipes,* right? What a misnomer *that* title is! I really enjoyed your book."

A bright red flush crept up Paisley's cheeks. Detective Leon was pretty cute. "Thank you."

"When can I look forward to the next one?"

"Oh, you know…"

"This might even make a good book. I'm so sorry," he said, concern suddenly clouding his dark brown eyes. "I shouldn't be making light of this. You could have lost your life."

"It's okay, really," Paisley reassured him. "I had no idea."

Detective Leon cleared his throat. He opened a file and pulled out a couple of photographs. "Do you know this woman?'

Paisley examined the image of the young blonde-haired woman. "No," she said, shaking her head. "I've met a lot of people, and I don't remember everyone I've met. I can't say definitely that I've never seen her before, but she doesn't look familiar, and I don't recall having met her."

"So you're saying that you don't know who she is."

"No. I don't know who she is."

"This is a young woman who was attacked by the man whose photograph I showed you – Jory Folker. He entered her place of residence while she was away and waited for her to return. He attacked her, put her in a garbage bag, and took her into a nearby wooded area. When he discovered she was still conscious, he attempted to knock her unconscious with a shovel. Then the assault ceased. She managed to work the bag off of her head, and she saw several crows attacking him. One of them had a white wing tag and leg bands that had the number 'ninety-nine' printed on them."

"Ninety-nine," Paisley whispered.

"She said the birds spoke to her, directed her to a ladder, and escorted her out of the woods to her home, where she called us."

"Wow." Paisley sat, stunned.

"When this young woman got the bag out off of her body, she saw that she was in what appeared to be a grave that Jory Folkner had dug previously."

"Oh my God!" Paisley covered her mouth with her hand, her brown eyes wide.

The detective pushed another photograph across his desk to her. "There was another freshly dug grave at the scene. This photograph was found at the bottom of it."

Paisley picked up the photo. Her hand trembled when she recognized her own face. "This was taken on my street, from just a few houses down. I'm gardening in front of my house."

Detective Leon nodded. "Based on the fact that we found this in the second grave at the scene, we have reason to believe that you were going to be Jory Folkner's next victim."

Paisley sat, silent with disbelief.

"We need to know if you remember anything, *anything* at all, about Jory Folkner. Did you ever speak

THE SHADY SIDE

with him? Did you ever see him interact with your neighbors? Did anyone ever visit him?"

Paisley thought. "I never even met the man. I saw him a few times, coming and going from his house, but that's pretty much it. I don't remember seeing him talking with anyone, or any visitors. When I saw him, he was by himself. I'm afraid I don't know very much at all."

* * *

Two days later, Einstein 99's photo was splashed across the front page of the local papers and online journals. The headlines all seemed similar: *"Kingfisher Lab Crow Foils Double Homicide"*, and *"Courageous Corvid Saves the Day"*, and *"Local Horror Author Saved by Pet Crow"*, and the saddest one of all: *"Faithful Crow Companion Loses Life While Attempting to Thwart Murderer"*.

Einstein received an award from the Mayor of Smith Mountain, and that photo appeared in the papers, as well.

Traffic backed up on quiet Laurel Avenue for three weeks as gawkers drove by, snapping photographs of Paisley and Einstein and anyone else that happened into the photo frame. Paisley's mailbox flooded with messages from well-wishers and readers, wondering where her next book was.

When the fervor had finally dwindled, Paisley sat on her front porch with Marjorie on a lazy August Saturday afternoon, sipping lemonade. A warm breeze stirred the foliage of the tree line beside the porch, where Einstein perched, blinking his one good eye sleepily.

"So what are you going to do now?" Marjorie's long silver chain earrings jingled as they brushed gently against her cheek, caught in the breeze.

"What do you mean, what I'm I going to do? What am I supposed to do?"

"I mean, are you going to move?"

"Why would I move?

"Well, I thought this street might have, you know, bad memories and everything, after…"

"After being targeted by a crazy serial killer madman? No, it doesn't. This is my home. I've lived here sixteen years. And nothing happened to me. I've had no bad experiences. Einstein got to him before anything happened." Paisley smiled fondly up at the crow, who held on to his branch effortlessly as it swayed gently back and forth in the breeze. "All the news was after the fact."

"But when you look down the street at that house, don't you get creeped out? I kind of do. And what about all the fans? Don't they bother you?"

Both women looked down the street at number 6 Laurel Avenue. The "For Sale" sign had returned to the front lawn. The windows of the brown ranch house were blank and empty, the lawn neatly mowed. All was quiet there.

"Why? There were no bodies found there. The guy barely lived there for four months. He was so temporary that I don't see a reason to be creeped out by it. And the readers? It was rough, there, for a few weeks, but it's calmed down. The only thing that bothers me about them is now people know who – and where - I am. I can't hide in anonymity anymore. My sales have skyrocketed – and now there is too much pressure to write another one like, really soon. But at least now I know they like my books."

Marjorie raised her hand and grasped the corner of her cat's eye sunglasses, lowering them so that she could look over the top of the rims with artfully made-up blue eyes. "I don't get how you can be so calm. If *I* found out I was the potential victim of a serial killer, I would be *so* freaked the fuck out."

THE SHADY SIDE

"Even if he got snuffed out and just kind of disappeared from the neighborhood, and you never even met him, barely ever even saw him?"

"Hell yeah, I would!"

Paisley smiled. "Well, we are two different people. But now that I think about it, it might make a good story. Maybe, *Eating Crow*."

Marjorie laughed, snorting. "Why do you make your books sound like recipe books? Why so food focused?"

"I can't help it. Zombies need comfort food, too."

"You're silly, Pais. Let's go smoke one."

Paisley laughed. "Now *that*, I can agree with."

THE END

Printed in the USA
CPSIA information can be obtained
at www.ICGtesting.com
CBHW060802300924
15126CB00001B/42

9 781732 179363